Never Too Late

Marjorie Cooke

Jeremy Books

5624 Lincoln Drive, Minneapolis, Minnesota 55436

Jeremy Books

5624 Lincoln Drive, Minneapolis, Minnesota 55436

NEVER TOO LATE

Copyright © 1980 by Jeremy Books

Printed in the United States of America

ISBN 0-89877-019-X

FOR HARLOW

Table of Contents

"Unless the Lord builds the house those who build it labor in vain."

—*the Psalmist*

CHAPTER I

Homecoming

With an audible sigh of relief, Edward Justin guided his car through heavy traffic to the off-ramp heading home. The blazing sun would soon set into the Pacific behind the bare California hills, and the heat of the spring evening seemed to subside as he slowed. Now there were oak trees and patches of green along the highway.

He pulled off his brown and orange tie and tossed it into the back seat, where it fell across one of the bulky packages. He smiled to himself as he unbuttoned the top buttons of his cream-colored shirt.

Jonathan would be seven on Monday, two days away. Edward knew the ball, mitt, bat, and glove would give them hours of pleasure together. The boy was quite good at sports for his age.

The other bulky package was a special hand-crafted doll cradle he had ordered to hold all of Aurora's dolls, including the soft cuddly one he had hidden in his suitcase. In fact, it would almost hold his small daughter.

The desire to see her was like a pain inside him.

He pictured her, just two, with silvery curls around her face, slightly tilted nose, generous mouth, and changeable green-blue eyes. Her brows and lashes were in dark contrast. Julia dressed her in soft colors, lace, and ribbons. People were always picking Aurora up to hug her and feel her ringlets curl around their fingers. The small girl responded with smiles and kisses. She behaved perfectly and everyone adored her.

There were times when he resented having to be away from his family so much, but God had given him the ministry of speaking and singing. He was asked to serve constantly. The past two weeks on the beach at Sea View Camp had been especially successful. He knew God was present, and he was thankful, but bone tired from lack of sleep, too much coffee, and too much rich food. The emotional strain and demands on his time had been rewarding but tiring.

He reached down and unbuckled his leather belt another notch. The camp cook had been a specialist at pastries and his weight gain was evident. Baseball would help, but not the planned night out on the town. He patted the folded brown suit coat on the seat beside him. In the pocket were two complimentary tickets to a special restaurant in San Francisco. He smiled. Julia would love the surprise.

It would be their eighth anniversary celebration. He knew she would curl her soft dark hair and put on a long dress—probably the blue jersey he liked—and look shapely and desirable, just for him. She was beautiful, with luminous dark eyes and glowing skin. It still amazed him how young she could look. But then, she was young. Just 27. She had finished high school the year he had finished college, and they were married immediately. Time had gone rapidly. He still loved her deeply and knew he always would.

The stop light blinked red. He became acutely aware of his surroundings as he responded and made a left turn to go through town on the main street.

Edward made a ritual of stopping on his way home to pick up a quart of soft ice cream to go with the berry pie Julia always baked for him. He could almost smell it already.

He slowed to a stop at the main intersection of Oakwood. Across the corner the evening sun painted the gray stone court house with its surrounding trees and gardens. His father had been mayor of the town for twenty-three years, and it was interwoven into every phase of Edward's life. He knew the town and its people intimately. Coming home was always a pleasure.

He missed his folks now that they were both gone, but they had left a rich heritage of hope and faith and love. They had enriched his life, and were active in their church and community. Many of their friendships endured even now, passed on to Edward and his family.

At the red and white ice cream parlor he chatted with several acquaintances and hurried on.

Near the south edge of town was the white two-story colonial home his father built, surrounded by gardens his mother planted. Edward, the only son, brought Julia here when his folks had died suddenly.

The street lights came on, and Mr. Kimball, their neighbor, waved to him as he picked up the evening paper the newsboy had tossed on the lawn.

Edward turned into his own driveway. The porch light was not on, and the living room windows showed no welcoming face. A touch of alarm made him shiver as he stopped in front of the unopened garage door.

At the first sight of the car Jonathan always came running and jumping to open the door and greet him noisily. Edward relished that first moment with his slim, dark-haired son.

There was no sign of movement from the house. All was dark except for a light in the kitchen. Maybe they were planning a special surprise.

He tapped the horn twice, the accustomed signal. Nothing happened. He got out and stood stretching, moving tired shoulder and neck muscles. He reached for the sack with the ice cream and shut the car door. He would get the gifts and suitcases later.

There still was no sign of movement from the house. He breathed a silent prayer as he went up the steps and opened the door to the back screened porch. Things seemed to be in order. He squared his shoulders and opened the door to the kitchen.

"Daddy! Daddy!" Aurora squealed from her high chair reaching her arms to him. She had a fresh scrubbed look in her pink pajamas and robe, kicking her feet in her bunny slippers.

He dropped the ice cream on the table and lifted her to him in a relieved and loving hug. Her tiny arms squeezed him, her sticky mouth kissed him, and she giggled delightedly.

Julia stood from her place at the table and came for his embrace. Strangely, her dress was wrinkled and stained. Her hair was uncombed.

"Edward, Dear, I didn't expect you so soon. What time is it?" She seemed confused and disoriented.

Unfinished pie ingredients were scattered on the counter. An uncooked roast stood in a pan on top of the oven.

"Please put Aurora down, Edward. I must finish feeding her and get her to bed. She's had a difficult day. Please don't excite her."

He put his tiny daughter back in her high chair. "What's wrong, Julia? Are you all right? Where's Jonathan?"

"Nothing, Dear. I'm fine. Just tired. Jonathan is sick. No, don't go and bother him. I just got him to sleep. He's had some medicine. Let me finish feeding Aurora. You get your bags in and relax—I'll fix dinner later. I'm glad you're home."

Aurora looked her usual adorable self. She bounced up and down showing her dimples and laughing at him. He patted her silver curls.

"Let me finish feeding her."

"No. I will. You go."

It was Julia who was not herself. Her movements were erratic. Her eyes were staring. Everything about her showed that something was very wrong.

Edward gave her a quick hug as he passed her chair. He decided it would be better to let her tell him in her own way. He put the melting ice cream in the freezer and went to the sink to fill the coffee pot. He covered the warm meat and put it back in the refrigerator.

Then he went to get his baggage and the gift packages and take care of the car. He made several trips, trying to be quiet because of Jonathan.

He crossed the hall to his son's room. The night light dimly revealed his face. Jonathan was sleeping deeply. Edward touched the boy's forehead but it didn't seem feverish. He wanted so much to wake him, but Julia had warned him not to and it might be best to wait until he knew what had happened. It did seem strange to see

Jonathan sound asleep so early in the evening. It wasn't like him at all, especially when he knew his dad was on the way home.

Edward was disappointed to miss the playtime he usually had with the children after being away from them so long. He had made a special effort to get here early enough, and he wanted to give them their gifts.

The usual relaxed feeling did not come as he shrugged into his old wool jacket. He changed to soft leather house boots. Anxiety clutched at his stomach. Something seemed terribly wrong.

In the kitchen, Julia was washing Aurora's face and hands. He waited to pick her up.

"No, Edward. I'm taking her up to bed. She has had enough excitement."

"But, Julia, it's early yet! I want to hold her!"

"You just don't know. I've given her two baby aspirin so she will go to sleep right away. You wait here."

He could not understand. The baby certainly looked normal, all full of twinkling smiles. She kept reaching toward him, trying to tell him something. None of her baby talk seemed to make sense.

Julia grabbed her out of the high chair and hurried through the swinging door.

Edward poured a mug of coffee and sat at the table with his hands cupped around it. Tiredness and hunger weighed him down. The gnawing pain in his stomach made him shift in his chair. He took off his glasses and rubbed the wrinkles above his eyes, pushing back his blond hair. He prayed for strength to face this crisis, whatever it was.

He had finished his coffee and was feeling better when Julia returned. She had combed her hair and changed into a hostess robe which outlined her lovely figure. But her fresh lipstick was on crooked, and her eyes still looked vague. She sank into a chair, ignoring the baby's empty dishes and dirty bib and tray.

Edward poured coffee for her and refilled his own cup. She sipped slowly, not meeting his eyes.

"Can you tell me now, Julia?"

Tears welled into her eyes. "Oh, Edward, it was so horrible!"

He moved his chair beside her and put his arm around her.

"She was covered with mud from head to toes . . . even in her mouth . . . mud . . ."

"Who? Aurora? Now, Honey, calm down. Start from the beginning."

She reached in her pocket and wiped her eyes on a wad of tissue. "I let Jonathan and Gary Kimball take the baby into the back yard while I was getting dinner ready. It is safe out there, and I can watch from the window. I could hear them, too. Then the phone rang. Mrs. Fromley was asking about the women's meeting next week."

She stopped and sipped her coffee.

"Julia, Jonathan has always been careful about taking care of Aurora. He loves her very much."

She looked at him. "Aurora was in her white pinafore, red dress, white shoes and socks . . . all ready for you. She looked so clean and beautiful. Then I heard her screaming. She just screamed and screamed. I ran to the window. I couldn't believe my eyes. When I got out there . . . you just wouldn't believe it . . . ."

"Now calm down. She's not hurt."

"No, but it is a wonder that she isn't dead. Jonathan and Gary had turned on the hose. I had dug up a small area this morning to plant some flowers. Aurora was sitting in the middle of that dirt. They had plastered her all over with mud . . . black filthy mud. It was even in her mouth. I couldn't believe my eyes. It was so horrible . . ."

"But, Honey, mud doesn't hurt . . ." His sense of relief nearly made him laugh.

Julia ignored him. "You should have seen her. I grabbed her and carried her in . . . dripping mud and water . . . and put her in the tub, clothes and all. I had to wash and wash . . . she spit and cried . . . and shivered . . . It was horrible."

"She wasn't hurt."

"Not physically . . . yet . . . it took a long time to calm her down."

"And Jonathan?"

"I spanked him. I put him to bed. He wouldn't shut up. I gave him a sleeping pill . . ."

Edward half-stood, alarmed.

"No, no, I mean, half of one. He was so upset. I had to stop his screaming . . ."

"But he is all right?"

"Yes, yes . . ."

"Now Julia, pull yourself together. Mud washes off. There is nothing wrong with good clean dirt. It's good for children to get dirty . . ."

"Edward, how can you say that? Disease comes from dirt. I have always been so careful. She will get sick . . . and die. I know she will! She is so special. I've always known she was too perfect for God to let us keep her. Now He will take her. I have been so careful . . ." She was crying uncontrollably.

He stood and pulled her to her feet, shaking her. "Julia, stop that at once."

She looked startled and relaxed into his arms. He led

her through the dining room and into the living room. He sat in the big chair and pulled her into his lap.

"Now, Honey, everything is fine. Few children get sick from eating dirt. I'm here now. I am sorry I have to be gone so much. You have always been so brave and capable. We can face this together. Everything is going to be fine."

His voice soothed her. She clung to him. At last she stopped crying and sat up. "Your dinner. You must be starving. Forgive me. I'll go . . ."

"We will both go and fix a snack. I'm sure we can find something."

After a quiet meal they went to bed. He held her in his arms, and soon she relaxed into a deep sleep.

Tired as he was, Edward remained awake. His home-coming had been different to say the least. He knew there was still something deeply wrong.

He slipped out of bed and went to look at his small daughter again. The nagging worry he had insisted on pushing clear to the back of his mind was forcing itself to his attention. Aurora was too coddled, too indulged, too spoiled. He would have to face this, and it was up to him to do something about it before another day passed, even though his peace-loving temperament made it diffi-cult for him to confront Julia, even when he felt she was wrong.

He prayed for wisdom as he straightened Aurora's pink satin cover and went again to his son's room. Jon-athan hadn't moved in his drugged sleep. He lay turned away from the dim light, his face pale in the dimness. Edward pulled a chair near the bed and sat with his head in his hands.

Jonathan was a sturdy, bright child. But . . . yes, it was true, he was neglected. Julia had been an excellent mother to him, but since the birth of their daughter only the necessary things had been done for the boy. Julia's whole life now centered on Aurora.

He could easily see why a boy and his friend would put mud on the perfect little girl with her frilly white pinafore and white shoes. He half-smiled. There had been times when he had wanted to do the same. She had never been allowed to come into contact with anything that wasn't freshly cleaned.

He sat up. "Face it," he thought to himself. "This is no way to raise a child. It is my fault, too. I must do something. I've got to find a way to be home more. I know God wants me to preach because He gave me a burden and the gift. But He has given me a family, too."

Jonathan groaned in his sleep and turned over. Something was wrong with his face.

Edward reached for the lamp and turned it on. The side of the boy's face was swollen and red. His eye was puffed shut. He had been beaten! Unbelieving, Edward pulled the covers back and lifted his son's pajamas. His back showed welts and streaks already turning blue. There were several places on his buttocks where the skin was broken and his pants were stuck with dried blood.

Gently, he felt over the child's body. Jonathan muttered and pulled away. Nothing seemed broken or out of place. He would have to be checked by a doctor in the morning. "How could I have missed how bad things were getting?" he asked himself. He felt numb with the realization.

Edward knelt by the bed and gently held the boy in his arms. Hot tears ran down his cheeks as he prayed. "Oh, God . . . Oh, God . . ."

The boy sensed his nearness and cuddled to him. Tears welled into his eyes and he shuddered in pain.

"Daddy . . . Momma . . . I didn't mean . . ."

"It's all right, Son. I'm here. We will talk later. You sleep now."

"I'm sorry, Daddy. I wouldn't hurt . . . Stay with me . . ."

Edward fell asleep on his knees beside the bed.

CHAPTER II
Grand Canyon

"How much farther is it, Jonathan? Can you tell where we are on the map?" Edward looked over at the boy sitting beside him in the front seat of the car. Julia and Aurora were in back.

"I think we're almost there, Daddy." The road map was folded open in his lap, the highway marked with a bright red pen.

Last evening in the motel they had talked it all over man-to-man while Julia bathed Aurora and tucked her into her own folding bed.

"Look, Daddy. The sign said Grand Canyon."

"And Yavapai Point. Shall we stop, Julia? Our first view of the canyon."

"It's four o'clock, Edward. I would much prefer to check in and get settled. Aurora will need her dinner soon."

Edward sighed, but kept moving. It wasn't worth getting Julia upset. They would see the canyon later.

Traffic was heavy; there were campers, trailers, and

cars full of excited people. Bicyclists with tied-on equipment and hikers of all ages surrounded them.

The road was now divided with colorful plantings. They had to slow down as a shuttlebus full of people pulled out in front of them.

"Can we ride in that, Daddy?"

"Of course, Son. It's free, too, and travels all over the park."

They passed the visitor center and the Shrine of the Ages. Both Edward and Jonathan wanted to stop, and a glance at each other communicated a promise to return at the first possible moment.

The old wooden railroad depot, no longer in use but carefully tended, was to the left. Near it were the horse and mule barns for those who rode the trails to the bottom of the canyon.

On the other side, driveways led up to a hotel and other new and beautiful motels. They were disappointed that there was no place to look into the canyon from the car.

They followed signs to the motor lodge where they had reservations. A sharp turn to the left brought them to an area of low trees and small cabins. A little farther on they saw the small building that housed the office. Across the street was a gift shop and cafeteria. People were coming and going everywhere.

Edward parked the car and turned off the key. He took off his hat and dark glasses and wiped his face with his handkerchief. The head was even worse now that they had stopped.

"I hope our rooms are air-conditioned," Julia said.

"We will soon see. Coming, Jonathan?"

"Me, too. Me, too."

"No, Love. You stay with Mama."

Aurora pouted charmingly, but Edward resisted her

chubby, outstretched arms as Julia took her.

More than an hour later, they were finally settled into their motel suite. Fortunately, they had a ground floor entrance.

Everything was luxurious. There was a spacious main room with a king-size bed, a smaller room with twin beds, and a large dressing and bath area. The rooms were air-conditioned and colorfully furnished with thick carpeting, orange and brown drapes in a geometric pattern and even a comfortable sitting area with a hanging lamp, low table, and four arm chairs. Julia was pleased.

Edward had promised himself that he would not complain about the mountain of supplies Julia had insisted on bringing. Every inch of the back of the station wagon was fully utilized. He lost count of the number of trips it took to carry things in for their three-day stay.

While Edward and Jonathan set up Aurora's bed in the smaller bed room, Julia took out the small hot plate and covered the dressing counter with supplies. She opened food for Aurora and put it on to heat. Then she bathed the baby and put her into her flowered pajamas and set her in the folding high chair.

"I'm awful hungry," Jonathan whimpered, as he leaned against his mother.

Julia started to push him away, but stopped when Edward cleared his throat. She rumpled his hair instead. "You and Daddy go to the cafeteria to eat."

"But, Momma . . . "

"No. I have some soup I'll heat for myself. I'll just stay here. It's cool, and besides, I'm tired."

Edward looked at her. She did look a bit wilted. "O.K., Honey, if that's what you want. Can we bring you anything?"

"No, thanks. You go on."

A sidewalk skirted the newer building, but beyond it they walked on the old broken cement and gravel road. The air smelled of pinon pine and juniper. The sun was setting but the heat was not diminishing. Jonathan skipped beside his father, obviously enjoying their companionship.

One-room cabins lined the road. They looked old. Small lean-to baths were attached to each house and they were heated by old fashioned wood stoves. Jonathan and his dad agreed that it would be more fun to stay in one of those and rough it.

Friendly, laughing people were everywhere. Doors were open and radios blared.

The cafeteria was immense and the food was inviting. Jonathan held up the line in his excitement over choosing from the variety of foods. He helped himself to a slice of melon, a dish of chocolate pudding, a piece of apple pie, and a hot dog. He smiled up at his dad as he took a carton of chocolate milk. Julia would not have approved of his selection, and Edward knew it. He decided to let Jonathan make his own choices, for once.

They carried their trays to a small table. Edward felt a sense of relief at not having Aurora with them. She always caused such a sensation. People noticed her and stopped to comment and enjoy her happy smile. Aurora loved it and showed off, wrinkling her small nose in a delightful way. Julia would beam, but Edward secretly detested it.

Edward had insisted that they take this trip together, hoping that it would help reunite and bring balance to the family. After several days of travelling, he had his doubts. Everything they had done, as much as he tried to avoid it, had centered around that small girl. Everything.

Jonathan was digging into his food, not taking time to talk. The black eye and bruised face had faded to yellow, green, and dark blue, but the body bruises were still tender. The hurt look in the boy's eyes, which made Edward ache inside, was there less and less as the days passed.

The doctor had yielded to Edward's pleas to not report the beating. The doctor had been his friend for years and seemed to understand. He promised to keep the incident on file and only report it if it happened again. Edward reassured him, and prayed it would never happen again.

Julia had tried to ignore the whole happening since Aurora showed no ill effects. Edward told her in no uncertain terms that she must never harm the boy again. He rarely raised his voice to her, and she had promised in tears to be kinder. She was honestly trying to show more affection and care for the boy.

The doctor had suggested a trip since it would be best to keep Jonathan out of school for a while. Edward had rearranged his schedule and Jonathan's teacher had given them some work to bring along. The boy and his father enjoyed reading together each evening.

Edward watched the cafeteria line thicken as a tour bus loaded with Senior Citizens arrived. He would have to wait for more coffee until they were finished.

"Coffee, Sir?" a waitress asked.

"Yes, please." Now he could enjoy his piece of pie.

"Hey, what happened to you, Son?" the waitress asked as she poured the coffee.

Jonathan ducked his head and hid behind his hand.

Edward said rapidly, "You should see the other kid. This boy is a tiger."

"I'll bet." She laughed as she walked away.

Edward lost his appetite.

"Daddy, I can't eat any more."

"O.K., Son." Julia would have scolded him for wasting at least half of the food he had taken. "Ready to go?"

On the way back Jonathan walked quietly along beside him carrying a small sack of breakfast rolls and a large chocolate bar, Julia's favorite.

It would be dark soon and he still hadn't seen the Canyon. Maybe Julia would walk with him. No, she would probably insist on staying with the children.

"You go in and get ready for bed, Son. Tell Mother I'm going for a walk. I'll be back soon. Okay? We'll work on that lesson then."

He watched the boy open the door and close it softly behind him. Then he turned and went back down the road past the cafeteria. It couldn't be far to the canyon rim.

He walked on and crossed the old rusted railroad tracks. Cars were parked on both sides of the road. He came to the barricade where the transfer point was made to the West Rim Shuttle. A bus was loading for the last trip up the canyon rim. The bus pulled out, leaving the odor of exhaust fumes.

A rock wall with a pipe railing ran along the top. He went to lean over it and look down into the canyon. He had seen pictures, but nothing had prepared him for the incredible vastness, depth, and color that spread before him.

Voices and sounds around him faded away completely. He felt alone and small and terribly insignificant.

"Oh, God . . . " he breathed. "God, thank you for this beauty."

No one could describe it. No artist could paint it. No photographer could do more than catch a moment of flatness.

Shadows were long, colors muted, distance deceptive. The sky was blue with white clouds picking up soft colors. An eagle soared, rising high on thermal currents, circling lazily, and then falling in rapid flight far below into the canyon.

His throat grew tight. Thoughts from the Psalms came flooding through his mind. And then the verse, "What is man that Thou art mindful of him . . . "

"Oh, God, how can You care for me and my insignificant problems?" But he knew deep inside himself that God did care. This mighty Creator cared for him and loved him.

He stood in worship and praise until darkness filled the depths below him. As he walked slowly back to his family his thoughts turned to their needs and he whispered a prayer for wisdom and courage.

Julia served instant cereal, rolls, hot drinks, and juice for their breakfast. They all laughed and chattered as they pitched in making beds and straightening the room. Edward's spirit soared. This was the way things should be.

"Now off to see the sights," he said, swinging Aurora high as she giggled delightedly.

"Not yet, Edward. I must get our things washed up. There's a laundromat near the market. I need to get some food, too. And some sun-tan lotion," Julia insisted.

"But Julia, we've come hundreds of miles to see this place . . . "

"All in good time, Dear. We have dirty clothes. Let me get caught up, then I can enjoy myself more."

The whole morning was spent with domestic duties, and then it was nap time. Edward sat in the motel reading as his family slept.

Preparation for the afternoon excursion was quite a production. Aurora was coated with suntan lotion and dressed in a ruffled pink sundress with a matching floppy brimmed hat. The pink stripes in Jonathan's tee-shirt matched Aurora's dress. Edward started to protest but Julia seemed so pleased with the effect. Even her dress had matching pink flowers.

They found a parking place at Yavapai Point and Jonathan proudly pushed Aurora's stroller up the wide sidewalk to the stone building.

Finally, the rested, neatly dressed family saw the canyon through an arc of windows. Edward helped Jonathan look through the series of telescopes and explained the exhibits and the large contour map of the canyon. The boy showed unusual interest and asked intelligent questions.

Finally Jonathan, tired of being indoors, went out the side door and he ran to the rock wall to look deep into the canyon. Edward protectively reached out to hold him as Jonathan leaned far over the rail. His eyes glowed. Edward put his hand on his son's shoulder, sharing the awesome moment.

"That little bit of blue way down there is the river?"

"Yes, Son. It's about sixty feet wide there and about forty feet deep."

"Look. A bridge. It looks like a tiny toy."

"That's the Kiabab Bridge and just there is Phantom Ranch. When you are older we should come back and hike down the trail."

"I can see part of it. Looks like a pencil mark. Wow!" He put his hand on his forehead. "I feel so little.

Oh look, a chipmunk. He's sitting up eating. Can I give him something?"

"We'll bring some food when we come back tomorrow."

Julia was sitting on a bench in the sparse shade of a stunted tree. Aurora sat in the stroller beside her, and several people were gathered around them. Aurora was smiling, wrinkling her tiny nose adorably. A man was setting his elaborate camera on its tripod, not to record the incredible view but to photograph the beautiful little girl!

A pain in Edward's stomach gripped him. He bent to hide his discomfort. He had a strong feeling that Julia had only glanced over the rock wall. Taking Jonathan's hand, he walked away along the gravel path and down a series of steps to another view point. The pain eased as he concentrated on his small son.

Later, in the motel, both children were asleep. Julia was curled in a chair looking at a magazine.

Edward stretched and yawned. "It's only nine o'clock. Too early to go to bed."

"Mmm, huh."

"How about a walk?"

She looked up.

"Oh, I know. We can't leave the kids. Let's just walk up and down outside. I found a set of old stone steps across the street in those trees. Used to be a lodge there."

"The children might call."

"We can leave the window open."

"The air conditioning?"

"Won't hurt for a short time. Come on, Julia. Your lounging pajamas look great. Please come."

"Bugs. It's hot out there."

"Please?" He took her hand and pulled her up and out the door.

They stood outside and breathed deeply of the warm spicy air.

"I love it," he said. "God seems closer here."

A few lights made circles in the semi-darkness, flickering as insects flew in and out. The stars were close and bright.

They walked across and into the trees. They sat close together on the stone steps that led nowhere.

"It's nice to be alone with you, Julia. How long has it been since I told you I love you?"

He kissed her, but she pulled away. Her eyes stayed fixed on the door of their motel suite.

"Honey, the children are safe."

"I can't help it if I worry."

"Can't you trust God to protect them?"

"Of course, but . . ."

"But what, Julia?"

"He gave them to us. They are our responsibility."

"We gave them back to God, Julia. They belong to Him, too."

"Oh, Edward, you always twist things. We have to take care of them here on earth."

"And God helps us."

"I know."

"Julia, you are doing better with Jonathan. But could you please not spend so much time with Aurora? You scarcely looked at the Canyon today."

"I saw it."

"Isn't it incredible! It's an experience just to see it. I'm so glad we came."

"The man who took pictures of Aurora promised to send us copies . . ."

"Julia, that is exactly what I mean. You care more about pictures of Aurora than enjoying this amazing place we have come so far to see."

"I do not."

"Don't you?"

"I can't help it, Edward. Our daughter is special. Everyone notices her."

"You are becoming obsessed, Julia. She is a cute little girl. Jonathan is a dear little boy. And I am a man who loves you and wants some of your time, too."

"Don't be silly."

"Julia, I'm serious. You have to stop devoting all your time to Aurora. You have to stop!"

She got up and walked away. He followed and took her arm.

"Listen to me, Julia. I hate to argue. This is important and I want you to listen to me." He took her in his arms. "Do you think if we had another child . . .?"

Her white face looked up at him in the dimness. "I don't know, Edward. Do I really spoil her?"

"You know you do."

"Oh . . . well . . . I'll try to do better."

Faintly they heard a child's call.

She was gone instantly.

He stood alone, shaking his head, his fists clenched.

CHAPTER III

Grace

"Julia, you're sure you won't change your mind and come with me?" Edward finished tying his tie and turned to her. "I hate to leave you here in the hotel alone."

She was dressed in a bright flowered robe and was sitting propped on pillows on the bed. "No, Edward. It is very cold out there. Since you are not the speaker at the convention this afternoon, I think I will just rest. You can visit with your friends more if I am not along. I get so tired if I stand too long. After all, the baby is eight months along and he's heavy." She smiled.

"I know, Dear." He sat beside her and kissed her lovingly.

"Edward, I wonder if the children are okay."

"Honey, you just called your mother this morning."

"I know, but I worry."

"Now, don't." He pulled her into his arms. "You are to relax and take care of yourself. Two active children are too much for you in your condition. That's why I brought you with me. I may have some news for you when I come back. Remember, I sent a letter asking for an interim pastorate near home? I have an appointment after the service. Keep your fingers crossed. I want to be home with my family all the time. Especially with the new baby." He patted her bulge lovingly.

"Yes, Dear."

"I've got to go. You rest. How about playing hooky and driving down to the beach this evening for dinner?"

He put on his overcoat, took his attache case, and left, throwing her a kiss from the door.

Julia flopped onto her side and hit at her distended belly with her fist. She hated it. She loathed the clumsy, stuffy feeling. The ache in her back drove her to distraction. Edward had confiscated all her pill bottles and warned her not to risk harming the baby inside her. She threw her magazines across the room.

Sometimes she hated Edward. Everything about him repulsed her. He was so smooth and undisturbed and peaceful. He never got angry or yelled, and he could talk her into anything. Now she was in this condition because he thought she spoiled Aurora!

Aurora spoiled? She laughed out loud. That lovely baby wasn't spoiled. She was just special—very beautifully special. All her own great musical talent was beginning to show in that child. She was singing in tune and humming constantly. She picked up melodies and could sing them after hearing them just once. At age three that was a miracle, a God-given miracle. Everything she had ever dreamed of doing or being was going to be hers through this beautiful child she had produced.

The thing inside her moved and pushed up under her rib, hurting her. She hit at it again. She hated it, too—everything about it. Now it was even keeping her from

Aurora—and Jonathan. He could take care of himself though, she thought. All boys could. Aurora? Would her grandmother really watch her? There was so much that could hurt a small child.

Four days ago they had left the children with Julia's mother in her tree-shaded home in the foot hills above Pasadena—four long boring days. The church Conference in Los Angeles would not be over for two more days. She was sick of going to meetings. The luxury hotel was supposed to be a special treat, but it was cold, impersonal, and much too quiet.

She rolled off the bed and stood, adjusting to the weight of the baby inside her. "Must be an immense monster," she thought. Her loathing increased as she saw her ungainly self in the full length mirror.

Edward's idea! Did he think keeping her from her baby would rest her? How utterly ridiculous! The more she thought about it, the madder she became.

Unzipping her robe, she stepped out of it, leaving it on the floor. She slid into the ugly flat shoes and the shapeless dress. Her coat barely closed over her tummy. She grabbed her bag and slammed out of the room.

Julia felt better when she was behind the wheel of the car. The doctor had advised her not to drive, but it wasn't too far, and nothing was going to keep her from her Aurora.

The early afternoon traffic was only moderately heavy. Following signs, she was soon on the Pasadena Freeway. Her spirits lifted. The February day was clear with only a little smog. The mountains held a slight dusting of snow on their topmost edges. The Mt. Wilson observatory dome reflected glints of light.

She reached the street lined with pepper and eucalyptus trees where her mother lived, and sighed with relief.

As she emerged from the car Jonathan came running toward her.

"Mom, Mom!"

He leaped at her in his joy, but she fended off his squeeze and gave him a brief kiss, looking for her daughter."

"Look, Mommie, look." Aurora came pedaling down the drive toward her on a huge new red tricycle. Her long curls were cut short and haloed her face. There was a scratch on her knee, and her dress was torn.

"Baby, be careful," she called, too late.

In her excitement Aurora misjudged the distance and slammed into the fender of the car. The tricycle tipped and threw her to the pavement head first where she lay unmoving. Blood began to well from a cut on her forehead.

Julia couldn't stop screaming as she fell on her knees beside the small child. "She's dying . . . get an ambulance . . . get a doctor . . . my Baby . . ."

Strong arms lifted her away. She struggled but it did no good. She couldn't see her baby. Several people were leaning over her.

A siren screamed as the emergency squad roared up.

"No danger, just a bump on the head. Will need a few stitches. No problem. She'll be fine," reassuring voices told Julia.

"Are you all right, Ma'am?" a young uniformed man asked.

"My baby?"

"I assure you, she will be fine. I suggest you take her to your doctor. We have checked her and put on a temporary dressing. Your doctor may want to take a few stitches and have you watch her closely because she was unconscious for a minute or two. However, children can take hard bumps. It's amazing. Ma'am?"

She suddenly felt dizzy. Then a knife-like pain cut through her. She doubled over and groaned.

Suddenly, she was the patient and found herself on a stretcher being examined. Another stabbing pain struck, and then she was in the ambulance with its shrieking siren.

The baby inside her was keeping Julia from comforting her injured daughter. She writhed in pain and frustration, feeling icy cold. Time blurred. In her mind she searched agonizingly for Aurora while many things happened to her body . . . voices, movement, wave after wave of pain, and finally, after untold agonies . . . sleep.

"Julia. Sweetheart."

The voice sounded far off. She pushed it away trying to ignore it.

"Honey, we have a girl. She's beautiful. Julia, we have a baby girl."

Her hand slid down under the covers to her stomach. The big heavy bulge wasn't there.

"Honey, she weighs four pounds and ten ounces. A daughter, Julia. I'm so proud of you."

She struggled out of her sleepy darkness. "I don't want her. Get rid of her."

"Julia?" He was leaning close and squeezing her hand so that it hurt.

"I want Aurora. Oh . . ." Remembering, she struggled to sit up.

He held her shoulders. "Aurora is all right, Dear. Believe me."

"I won't. I have to see her. She's hurt. She's dying. Let me up. I have to go . . ."

A nurse pushed a needle into her, and the hysterical woman's struggling surrendered to a drugged sleep.

When she awoke she lay with her eyes shut a few minutes, trying to keep out reality. The baby was born and no longer inside her—at least that was a relief! But she had no desire to see her, and refused to give her the morning feeding. She laughed when the doctor asked her if she planned to nurse her. The nurse kept checking her and bothering her.

Aurora was fine, everyone told her, but she didn't have long curls any more. Her grandmother must have cut them. She had no right! She would never forgive her. Now her daughter had stitches on her face. A scar! She couldn't bear it. Would they lie to her? Who could she believe? Maybe her angel child was dead. She had to know. She reached for the bedside phone and dialed her mother's number.

"Hello?"

"Mother, how could you?"

"Julia, how are you? We are so happy about the new baby."

"You cut her hair!"

"Oh, Aurora? Calm down, Dear. She did it herself. She got the scissors and chopped at it. I had to trim it off even. We like it short. How are you, Dear?"

"Mother, I have to know about Aurora."

"She's fine. I had to lock up the tricycle. She insists on riding on it."

"I don't believe you!"

"My Dear, just a moment." Faintly Julia heard her ask Jonathan to call his sister.

"Mother, tell me about her head."

"Three stitches. They won't even show. They're on the hair line. After it grows back in no one will ever know."

"Grows back in? They shaved . . ."

"Just a small area. She is so proud of herself. Here, Aurora, say hello to Mommie."

"Hello."

"Angel, Baby, are you all right?"

"Mommie, I have bandage. Can I ride bike, please?"

"No, Aurora. You stay off of it."

"Yes, Mommie. I love you. Come home."

"I love you, too, Baby. Is Jonathan there? Hi, Son."

"Thanks for the sister, Mom. When can I see her? I love you, Mom."

"I love you, Son." She hung up, surprised to realize that she really did love him.

Now she would have to get out of here. She had learned her lesson. She would never trust Aurora with anyone again.

How soon would the doctor let her leave? She called the nurse.

Hospital routine took over. She ate breakfast and took a short walk. They asked if she would like to see her new daughter. She consented, trying to hide her reluctance.

The tiny baby was placed in her arms. Julia stared down at the small face, eyes closed in sleep. She was surprised by her long dark lashes and a dark fuzz of hair. She touched her tiny nose and lips. They puckered and she opened her eyes.

Julia thought to herself, "I didn't want you and I thought you would be an ugly monster, but you're not so bad! Not pretty like Aurora was, but not bad. I'm glad you aren't ugly."

Later Edward came in with the doctor.

"How are you, Dear?"

"Fine. I want to go home."

"No reason you can't, Mrs. Justin. I will arrange it.

You had a good delivery, and the baby is strong and well. You both have much to be thankful for."

Edward nodded. "You are so right. Thank you, Doctor."

"Mrs. Justin will need help for a few days."

"We plan to stay in Pasadena with Julia's mother for a week or two before we go north."

"Good. I will arrange everything. You should be able to leave after lunch. Excuse me."

"Thank you, Doctor. Julia, Love, our daughter is so beautiful. You did such a good job."

"Yes."

"Have you thought of a name for her?"

"No. You choose one."

"I did think of one ... plain ... old fashioned. How about Grace and Maria after my mother? Grace Maria Justin."

"That's fine."

"Julia, are you all right?"

"Yes. Just get me out of here. I want to go ... home."

CHAPTER IV
Mrs. Greeley

Rev. Edward Justin kneeled at the wooden altar rail, his head in his arms. The ache inside him wouldn't go away now, and at times sudden, stabbing pains made him catch his breath. He should see the doctor.

He thanked God for his call as interim pastor to this small church in Pleasant Valley. He sat back on his heels and looked around him at the small frame structure with seating for about one hundred and fifty. The wood-paneled interior, carved pews, rail, and the rostrum all revealed someone's loving and artful touch. The center front contained a variety of woods which contrasted beautifully with the waxed and polished inlaid cross. A deep blue carpet emphasized the blue shadings in the stained glass windows. The afternoon sun was shining through the windows, filling the room with the glory of God's presence.

All the prayers within Edward welled into one poignant, aching cry mixing thanksgiving and his deep need. He prayed aloud for strength to guide him as he pastored this congregation, and he prayed for himself, for help with his insurmountable family problems.

The words from the Book of Timothy kept coming into his mind. "If a man can't manage his own family, how can he take care of the church of God?"

He prayed for Julia. He was thankful that she participated eagerly in church activities and he sensed that the music and women's departments benefitted by her presence. Now they could share a church family—something they had missed when he travelled so much.

At home, she expended her energies on keeping the house in order and making Aurora happy. Jonathan was cared for as a necessity. But even worse, Grace was neglected.

Dearest Grace. A precious gift from God. He prayed, "Please, God, help Julia love our baby."

He thought of Jonathan. Their times together were special, and they were close friends. It was getting more and more difficult for Jonathan to get along with Aurora. He prayed for his son and for his daughters.

Then he prayed for himself. The time demanded of him to adequately serve the growing congregation was increasing with a slow, steady growth. On top of that, money was becoming a problem. Expenses at home were increasing alarmingly. Julia's spending sprees were uncontrollable. What could he do?

She only listened to him when she felt like it.

Arguments and discord tied him in knots. He must go to a doctor. The pain inside must be checked. He knew he had brought it on himself. He hated conflict. No doubt his mother and father had argued, but never in his hearing. As he grew up, home had been a happy and peaceful retreat.

Loving Julia no longer seemed to be enough. The uncertainty of her moods, her sudden bursts of anger, and her habit of seeming to listen and then doing as she pleased, were overwhelming him. He knew he could be more assertive, but it meant so much unpleasantness.

"God, forgive me and help me," he prayed. He stayed on his knees, head bowed in quietness. Scripture verses he had memorized long ago came to mind to comfort him. Edward rose from his prayer time with a renewed sense of peace. God would use these hard times to bring growth. He could face the challenge.

He stopped by the small room that served as his study and the choir room. His Sunday sermon was prepared, but he would take it home and go over it again this evening. Edward cleared the top of his desk and turned the key to lock it. A knock sounded on the outside door, and he went to answer it.

"Pastor Justin?" A familiar face greeted him. The woman was tall and dressed neatly in a dark suit. Her black hair was threaded with strands of silver, and laugh wrinkles outlined her warm brown eyes. Mrs. Esther Greeley was one of the most faithful attenders, but she had never been to see Edward before. He wondered what the problem could be.

"Yes. Do come in."

"I've been trying all day to work up courage to come." The pastor prepared himself to listen patiently. "Someone told me that you are looking for a housekeeper." She sat gracefully on a chair and folded her hands over her black leather bag.

"Yes, I am." He surprised himself. Only now did the thought enter his head as a possible answer to his domestic situation.

"I really do not need to work, but I was praying about my loneliness and the idea stuck in my mind. My husband has been gone over a year. My family is grown and scattered. I would like to be of service to someone, but I have no references. I've never worked for anyone before."

"This sounds perfect, Mrs. Greeley. However, there are several special problems which would necessitate utmost discretion. I would have to trust you to be very positive and . . ."

"Oh, I'm not a gossiper, Reverend."

"Exactly." He smiled and leaned back in his desk chair pushing up his glasses. "It would not be easy. I have three small children. My wife is not well enough to handle all the household details."

"I have five of my own and six grandchildren. I love children. I guess that is why I am so lonely. I am so used to having them around."

"Could you live with us? I know that is asking a lot, but we would like to have you as part of our family. I would leave it to you and my wife to work out details. As to salary . . ."

"I would require very little. I have my own home and my husband left me quite well fixed. I would consider my position with you as a service to God, and to you and this church. I have attended here all my life."

"Mrs. Greeley, you are too good to be true. Could you come with me now to meet my family?"

"Why, yes, but I have my car. I will follow you, save you an extra trip."

He picked up the phone and called Julia. "I am bringing a guest, Dear. No, don't worry. I will pick up food for dinner as I come through town. We'll have a picnic."

As Mrs. Greeley followed in her car, he noticed she was a competent and careful driver. He liked everything about this woman and thanked God for such an obvious answer to prayer.

Jonathan was in the driveway to meet the horn signal as he drove into the open garage. By the time he got out and hugged his son Mrs. Greeley was there, and he introduced them.

"Hello, young man," she said, holding out her hand.

Jonathan squared his shoulders and stood tall as he shook hands with her.

They got the packages of food out and carried them in. Julia was embarrassed to greet her guest at the back door but regained her poise as they entered the kitchen. She wished that she had had the time to take care of the dirty dishes and signs of breakfast and lunch on the counters, sink, and table, but she walked by them now as if they weren't there.

Four-year-old Aurora was sitting in her youth chair at the table looking spotless and beautiful with a white dress and freshly combed curls. She smiled at Edward and Mrs. Greeley.

"I hope you don't mind. I thought it best to go ahead and feed Aurora," Julia explained as she turned to the little girl. "Greasy food isn't good for her."

"Where is Grace?" Edward asked.

"In bed, of course. It's time to feed her, too; but she's quiet, for once. Never bother a quiet child, you know," Julia said, smiling.

"May I help set out the food? Could we just eat here in the kitchen?" Mrs. Greeley was asking as Edward pushed through the swinging door to hurry upstairs.

The fourth bedroom had become Grace's room. It was completely bare, except for her crib and a small chest of drawers. Because it was a large room, it would be easy to put in a partition to give Mrs. Greeley her own private place.

He switched on the light. His year-old daughter lay

cross-wise at the bottom of the crib completely un-
covered. There were tear stains on her cheeks, and a tear
drop was caught in her long dark lashes. She was asleep
sucking her thumb. The odor made it obvious that she
needed changing.

Jonathan had followed him. "I tried to help her,
Daddy, but I couldn't. I was just going to get her a bottle when I heard you coming."

"It's all right, Son. Thank you. Would you please
ask Mrs. Greeley to come up here?"

She came immediately and stood beside him. Grace
opened her eyes and looked up at them. They were large
and clear blue in her thin white face. The corners of her
mouth turned up showing dimples as she saw her
Daddy.

"Reverend, you certainly do need me." Mrs. Greeley
picked up the smelly baby and hugged her. Her expression acknowledged her complete understanding. "Jonathan, you show me where things are, and we will clean
up this little darling and take her down to join the
party."

A lump of thankfulness choked Edward as he turned
to go back down stairs. If only Julia would accept this
help in the right spirit.

"Oh, Edward, look at all the lovely things I bought
in town today. They had sales everywhere," Julia said,
coming into the dining room. The table was heaped with
bags and packages. "Look. Isn't this adorable?" She
held up a fuzzy blue coat with lace edging on the collar
and cuffs. "Oh, I got some things for Baby Grace and
Jonathan, too," she quickly added as she noticed Edward's expression.

"Julia, Mrs. Greeley will move in and help you with

the children and the house, if you wish."

She looked at him in amazement. "You mean . . . a housekeeper . . . I'm not . . . I don't. . . . "

"Now, Honey, just think it over. You haven't been too well since Grace was born. She would take care of Grace and do whatever house work you wanted her to do. By the way, who baby-sat while you went shopping today?"

"Oh, Jonathan, I kept him home from school this afternoon. His teacher doesn't mind. I took Aurora with me."

"Julia, I told you not to do that again. A nine-year-old is too young for that kind of responsibility."

"Well, he can always go next door to the Kimball's for help. And it was a very special sale. Look, Edward . . ."

"Honey, later. We have a guest. We are all hungry, and the food is getting cold."

"Oh, I'm sorry."

"Will you think about having Mrs. Greeley help us for a while?"

"I wouldn't think of letting her black hands touch . . ."

"Julia! Don't you ever say anything like that again." He pushed up his glasses ignoring the sharp pain in his stomach. He tried to speak calmly. "Just think it over, will you?"

"Yes, Edward." She was rigid with anger.

Jonathan came bouncing down the steps, followed by Mrs. Greeley carrying Grace in a clean pink sleeper. The baby looked so sweet with her dark, fine hair framing large blue eyes and tiny tilted nose. She reached toward her Daddy. He took her and hugged her closely.

His eyes thanked his new, kind friend for her understanding.

When they went into the kitchen Aurora had scattered a box of cereal, left on the table since breakfast, all over the table and the floor.

"Oh, Sweetheart," Julia said rushing to her. "Did you want some cereal? I'll fix it for you."

"No, Momma." She jumped down from her chair crunching the cereal under her feet. "I want some of that." She ran over and tried to reach the sacks of food on the back of the counter. A dish crashed to the floor breaking nearly in half.

"All right, Dear. Come sit in your chair and you shall have some."

Jonathan got the dust pan and broom without being told and Edward swept the floor. Mrs. Greeley sat with Grace cuddled in her lap.

Finally they were all fed. Aurora refused to eat anything but a huge pile of French fries. Mrs. Greeley had warmed cans of fruit and meat and vegetables for Grace, and she ate it eagerly.

"More coffee, Mrs. Greeley?" Edward asked.

"Just a bit, thank you. I must get home."

"I want to sing for her," Aurora insisted.

"What a lovely idea," Julia said, forgetting about the coffee. "Daddy hasn't heard your new song yet. Come. Let's go to the living room."

She took Aurora's hand and led the way. She swept up an armload of newspapers from the couch, some toys, a pile of books from the piano bench, and dumped them all between the wall and the grand piano. She slid onto the bench and skillfully ran her fingers through a series of difficult scales and chords.

Aurora pulled a small footstool near the piano and

climbed on it. She posed with folded hands, smiled at each of her audience, and said, "I'm ready now."

Edward shuddered inwardly. Jonathan came to lean against his leg, and Edward put his arm around him. Mrs. Greeley held Grace while she contentedly took her bottle.

As much as Edward disliked the exploitation of his daughter, he had to admit that she was gifted. Her voice was pure and clear and had an amazing range. He knew it was remarkably mature for so young a child.

Julia was a different person at the key board. She always claimed that she had given up a concert career to marry Edward. He knew better. She had never had the drive or dedication needed for that kind of success.

As Aurora sang, Edward tried to shove away the fear that this gift of hers could develop into something much too involved for him to handle.

Mrs. Greeley tucked the baby into her clean bed before she left. Edward walked to the car with her.

"I have no right to ask you to get involved in my problems," he said.

She put her hand on his arm. "Reverend, I love a challenge. It is great to be needed. Please let me help you."

"Thank you. I will do my best to convince Julia. Thank you for coming into our lives. You are an answer to prayer. I will hope to have some definite plans in mind when I see you tomorrow after church."

"I'll be there."

CHAPTER V
Christmas

Edward drove out of the hospital parking lot feeling amazingly well. Johnny Jensen's fracture was healing nicely. Mr. Moore was recovering from his heart attack. Best of all, his own tests showed great improvement. His stomach hardly ever gave him a twinge.

Now he could concentrate on the Christmas activities at church and at home.

Things had gone so smoothly at home since Mrs. Greeley had moved in. What a God-send she was, and he was extremely thankful. Julia was so much better. She had become even more interested in church activities and was accompanying and playing the organ and piano regularly. She was leading a women's group. She was even sincerely trying to keep her spending sprees under control, and did well until Aurora's fifth birthday came along. Her party had been a major production.

He slowed to a stop and then made a right turn.

According to Julia, the party had been a great success, but it had left him with a headache as he tried to balance the check book. He feared what Christmas shopping would do to the bank account. As usual, her allowance for Christmas gifts had been spent the first day and he was sure she was deep into the charge account. They would have to have another discussion. Sometimes he wondered what life would be like if Julia were content with less. His salary could never cover all the luxuries she craved. Edward decided that he would have to close their charge account, but he knew that she would be furious. He dreaded the confrontation.

He shrugged his tired shoulders and tried to stop thinking about their financial problems.

The sun was setting, reflecting shades of pastel orange, pink, and gold on the fluffy clouds. The air was clean and cold, promising frost. The trees were black against the sky and cast their skeleton-like shadows in dark patterns. Every season was beautiful in northern California.

As he drove through town, a glance at the clock in front of the drugstore reminded him that he would have just enough time to grab a bite to eat, shower, and get his family back to the Christmas program. Mrs. Greeley had offered to drive them and save him a trip home, but he preferred it this way.

He smiled to himself as he thought of Baby Grace. She would be two in February, such a cute age with her chubby struggles to stand and walk. She was quiet and good-natured, a happy child—thanks to Mrs. Greeley. The girls at church all would be glad to hold her tonight.

Jonathan met the car as usual with open garage doors and welcoming light.

"Hi, Dad. Do I have to be a shepherd?"

"Hey, Son, that's an honor, remember?" He made a playful pass at him with his fist as they went in the back door. Jonathan dodged skillfully.

"But, Dad . . ."

"Oh, come now. We've gone over all this a dozen times."

"I know but . . ."

"You were still hoping."

"Right."

"Did I ever tell you about the time I was a wise man and lost my robe . . ."

"Yes, Dad. Several times."

"You'll live through it, believe me. How about us doing some Christmas shopping tomorrow? Let's go to San Francisco."

"Wow! For all day?"

"Why not?" The idea excited them both.

"Welcome, Reverend." He couldn't break Mrs. Greeley of calling him that.

"Da-dee, Da-dee," Grace called from her high chair. He kissed her sticky face and felt her messy hands on his neck. Her skill at feeding herself left a lot to be desired.

"I know we're in a hurry," Mrs. Greeley said, "so I fed the rest. Here is a bite for you." She set a bowl of savory stew at his place at the table. She added warm rolls and a fruit salad.

He washed his hands at the sink and sat down. Jonathan sat beside him, and Mrs. Greeley slid a glass of milk and a plate of cookies to him. She finished feeding Grace and took her to clean her up. She and Grace were wearing new clothes to honor the occasion.

"Shouldn't you get ready, Son?"

"Just gotta grab my dumb costume. Can't get near the bathroom anyhow with all that dressing up Mom and Rora are doing."

"Dressing up?"

"You should see. All she has to do is stand up and

sing 'Away in a Manger.' Mom has been in a dither all day."

"Why?"

"She decided Rora should be dressed like an angel so she's been sewing madly and making wings and all."

"Oh, no."

"Yeah. Big deal! Her first public performance . . . I'm so sick of hearing them practice that dumb song I could . . ."

"I bet."

"Hey, Dad, let's go to San Francisco now."

"Jonathan . . ."

Edward tried to look stern as he stifled a smile.

"Yeah, okay. Hope Mom finished my costume."

"Better go see, Son." He piled his dishes in the sink and cleared things away. He would get his clothes and shower in the basement.

Upstairs, all was complete confusion. Julia was flitting around in her slip. Aurora was standing on a chair in the bathroom in her panties, screaming at Julia to hurry.

"Oh, you're home at last," Julia said pushing past him. "I just got Aurora's hair dry. We've just got a few more minutes. Better hurry." She almost tripped over the dryer cord.

"Honey, calm down. Plenty of time. Aurora, you hush." She looked at him and screamed louder.

He went to her and lifted her off the chair wrapping her robe around her. She was stiff in his arms, but she stopped screaming.

"Put her down, Edward. I must dress her."

"Hey, Mom," Jonathan said coming into the hall. "My costume isn't sewed." He held the pieces of brown cloth in his hands.

"I just didn't have time." She held the white gauze and silver angel dress up to admire it.

"What'll I do, Dad?"

"Julia! . . ." Edward was appalled at her insensitivity.

"Oh, Edward, hush. I've got too much to do. Get Mrs. Greeley to do it." She slid her own new red dress carefully over her head and backed up to Edward to have it zipped. She checked her hair in the mirror.

"You know she doesn't have time. Why didn't you . . ."

"I just didn't get to it. Here, Angel, let's put this on. Now stand still."

"Julia . . ."

"Oh, go away, both of you." She slipped the delicate costume carefully over Aurora's silver curls.

Edward saw his daughter screw up her face and stick out her tongue at Jonathan. The boy reached over and pinched her on the arm.

There was a ripping sound as she jerked away. She opened her mouth and screamed.

Julia whirled and slapped Jonathan across the face. He staggered, almost fell, and stood glaring. He turned, ran down the stairs, and out of the house.

It had happened so fast Edward couldn't believe what he had seen.

"Baby," Julia said comforting Aurora by rubbing the slightly red place on her white arm. "Did he hurt you, Love? What a naughty brother. There is just a tiny tear in your dress. I can fix it in a jiffy. Now you must stop crying, or you will damage your lovely voice."

Edward stood, fists clenched. He wanted to slap both Julia and Aurora. Instead, he turned and walked down the steps, grabbing his overcoat and Jonathan's hat and jacket as he left. He had to find his son. He picked up a piece of brown cloth that was lying in the driveway.

Should he take the car? Where would a ten-year-old boy go on a cold dark winter night with no jacket?

He got the electric lantern from the shelf in the garage and then, carrying his son's hat and coat, he started walking up the street.

He beat down the hurt inside him seeing again his son's angry eyes and red marked face. He had to be found and comforted.

The church program. They would expect their pastor to be there. He had responsibilities—the benediction, lead singing, take a collection, make announcements, and help with the children's treats.

Nothing but his son was of importance now. His son. "Oh, God . . ."

He began to call. The street lights made dim circles in the cold darkness. A dog barked angrily at him through a picket fence. Someone yelled at it. Another dog began to follow him, yapping at his heels. He turned and aimed a kick at it. The dog ran from him, howling, even though he hadn't touched it.

He stood at the corner looking around. The few street lamps were not enough to cut through the black darkness. Night sounds were muted: music, car engines, a siren in the distance.

Where would a boy go? A hurting boy? One who wouldn't want to see anyone?

The park? He walked rapidly the several blocks. Anxiously he followed the gravel paths, calling. No one.

The school? Again, he almost ran the two blocks and circled the building searching and calling. His small light showed nothing.

He stopped running and stood on the curb looking up and down the street. A police car slowed to a stop.

"Something wrong, Sir?" One of the men got out and stood beside him.

"My son. He ran out of the house. I can't find him."

"How long ago?"

He glanced at his watch. "Almost an hour."

"Well, Sir, you give us his description. We'll watch for him. If he doesn't turn up soon, call us and we will organize a search. Why don't you try at home? He has probably gone back there by now. It is cold and dark, and I see you have his jacket."

Edward nodded his thanks. They took the boy's description: ten years old, blond hair, blue eyes, thin face, blue slacks and V-necked sweater, white shirt, black dress shoes.

They drove off, and he turned toward home. His eyes burned; his stomach ached agonizingly. He prayed aloud, the words catching in his throat.

The lights of the house were visible from down the block. Mrs. Greeley's car was gone. She must have taken the family to church. He hoped so. He couldn't face Julia now.

Then he remembered the tree house. Of course. On the back corner of a nearby vacant lot was an immense oak. The neighborhood boys had nailed boards high in its branches to make a club house. He stood beneath it shining the light up.

"Jonathan?"

He heard a faint scraping sound.

"Son, please come down. We need to talk."

No response.

Setting the electric lantern on the ground, he looked up at the boards nailed cross-wise at strategic intervals between limbs. It had been ages since he had climbed a tree. He hoped the boards would hold him. He kept hanging Jonathan's hat and jacket above him as he progressed.

He reached the platform and sat, panting, on the edge of it.

Jonathan's face stood out in the darkness as he lay curled tightly, shivering.

"Here, Son. Your jacket and hat." He helped the boy into them and pulled him into the circle of his arms. He put his face against his son's and felt tears on both.

What could he say? What was there to say?

"You shouldn't have pinched her, Son."

"I know, Dad. I couldn't help it. She follows me everywhere. She is always bugging me. When Mom isn't there she's . . . she's awful. My friends go away. She . . . she . . . Oh, Dad . . . And Mom doesn't like me."

"I'm sorry your mother hit you. I told her to never do that again. Has she done it before? Since . . ."

"She pushes me away. She says I bother her. She yells. But she hasn't hit me since . . ."

Edward took a deep breath. The darkness shut them in. The dry leaves made whispering sounds. It was a moment he would never forget.

"Son, we have to try to understand. We are the men of the family, and we have to be strong. I know your mom seems unfair sometimes, but she isn't well right now. Please keep loving her."

How could he make this small boy understand when he couldn't himself? Oh, God . . .

"You see, your mother, she is special. When we married she had dreams and hopes . . ."

That was too difficult to explain.

"You see, Jonathan, she sees herself in Aurora. Aurora has special gifts of beauty and musical talent. Those are God-given, and your mother sees them as a special responsibility. She feels that she must help develop them and see that Aurora uses her abilities correctly . . ."

"Mom spoils her. She lets her do anything." The boy was still shivering.

"That is where we must help. We must be strong and try to help Aurora think of others as she gets older. We have to be very wise. Can you understand, Son?"

"I think so. But . . . but Mom doesn't even love Grace and me . . ."

"You're wrong, Son. She does, but her desire to make Aurora successful has become so important to her that she . . ."

"But she doesn't even need us or want us . . ."

An overpowering urge shook Edward to the depths of his being. He sat gasping, clutching at his son. He desired beyond thought to climb down, pack their things, and leave. He wanted to go and make a new life, forget his obsessed wife and his too-beautiful daughter Aurora with her golden voice. Let them manage. They would. Julia would see to that.

He could trust Mrs. Greeley to take care of Grace until he could send for her. Why not? It would be so easy . . .

He shivered, thinking wildly.

Get down. Pack for himself and Jonathan before Julia came home. Leave . . . drive . . . anyplace. Find a small town. Get a job as a car mechanic . . . he had always wanted to do that . . . or a farm hand . . . or a construction worker. A place to work with his hands. A peaceful place with no conflict.

He hugged Jonathan tighter and shivered. Would he, could he leave God and his calling? Leave the responsibilities of church and family? Leave God after all His great gifts and blessings?

Jonathan began to cough and cry. It was as if Edward heard a trap in his head spring shut with an audible sound. He had to go home. There was no escape. God help him.

Stiffly, slowly, carefully, they climbed down and walked home arms around each other.

* * *

The boy had at last fallen asleep after he had worked with him a long time, feeding him, bathing him, giving him cough medicine, talking to him, loving him. He sat exhausted in his deep chair in the living room.

Edward heard a car come into the driveway. Doors slammed and Aurora came running in and jumped into his lap. Excitement glowed from every inch of her.

"I did it, Daddy. It was gorgeous. Everyone said so!"

Julia followed, her eyes stormy. "How could you desert us, Edward? We were almost late. No one could understand why you weren't there. You missed Aurora's performance. She was perfect. How could you not come? Why didn't you bring Jonathan? I hope you spanked him. Come, Baby. You must get to bed."

"I'm hungry, Momma."

"O.K., Sweety. We'll have some warm cocoa."

Edward just stood shaking his head, heartsick.

Mrs. Greeley paused on her way upstairs with Grace asleep in her arms.

"Let me take her," Edward said. "She's pretty heavy for you."

"Thank you. Is Jonathan all right?"

"I found him. He's asleep."

"How is he?"

He shrugged. He placed his small, warm daughter in her crib and watched as Mrs. Greeley changed her and put her into her sleeper. She wakened only enough to smile up at him. He bent to kiss her.

"Reverend, it was a fine program. The Sunday school superintendent handled everything skillfully when I told him you had an emergency."

"Thank you."

"Aurora sang beautifully."

"I'm sure she did."

"Julia was so proud."

"I'm sure."

She put her hand on his arm. "I'm sure it will work out."

He couldn't answer her and stared at the floor.

"I'm sorry I have to leave. My train leaves early in the morning. My children expect me to be with them over Christmas. I hate to leave. I'm sorry."

"It is all right, Mrs. Greeley." He looked at her with gratitude for her understanding. "You go and have a good time. You have done so much for us."

"I'll pray for you."

"Thank you." He went back and sat in his chair in the living room in the dark until he was sure Julia was asleep.

CHAPTER VI
School

Edward woke suddenly with the early autumn sunlight shining directly in his face. How could it be nine o'clock? The flu had really sapped his strength.

He stretched and yawned, feeling amazingly well. His headache was gone and his stomach was rumbling from emptiness. The light-headed feeling came momentarily as he sat up, reminding him that he was not completely well. Edward showered and dressed slowly.

Faint sounds came from downstairs. Holding onto the railing, he descended the stairs, passed through the dining room, and entered the kitchen.

"Good morning, Reverend. I was just going to bring your breakfast. How do you feel?"

"Much better, thank you."

Grace was sitting in her high chair eating small pieces of dry cereal. She looked up and started chattering at him. He picked her up, hugged her, and sat at the table, holding her on his lap. She smelled so clean and was so happy. He kissed her on the neck, enjoying her giggles.

Mrs. Greeley brought his breakfast and sat to have coffee with them while he ate.

Grace wiggled down. "Daddy, eat." She climbed back into her chair.

Their peaceful interlude ended abruptly as a car drove into the drive, doors slammed and Aurora came running in, followed by Julia.

Aurora's face was tear-stained and red, but she was smiling. "I want some cookies," she demanded.

Julia looked pale and grim. She took off her coat and sat dejectedly. "I just can't leave her there at school. She hates it so much. She screams and cries."

"This is the third day you have taken her and then brought her home," Edward said. He had been too sick to care before today.

"I know. It's such a traumatic experience for such a little girl," Julia said, hugging Aurora close to her. "This is her first time away from home."

"I hate it. I hate it," Aurora stamped her foot, her silver curls dancing. There was a triumphant gleam in her green eyes. She was stuffing cookies into her mouth.

"Aurora, come here." Edward made her stand directly in front of him and held both her hands in his. "You are five-and-a-half years old. You are a big girl. You are going to kindergarten and you are going to stay there. Do you understand?"

Tears welled into her eyes. "I can't, Daddy. I'm afraid . . ."

"Aurora, you listen to me."

"I won't go. I won't go." She stamped her foot and shook her curls around her angry face.

He turned her over his knee and spanked her hard several times. She was too startled to cry at first, but then she roared.

Julia stood, horrified. "Edward . . . "

"You be quiet," he told Julia. "Now, young lady, you stop that crying and listen to me. I am going to take you back to school. You are going to be good and do everything the teacher tells you. If you don't, I'll spank you again."

She caught her breath and rubbed her bottom. This was a new experience, and she looked up at him. He was frowning. "Okay, Daddy."

He took her hand and led her to the car. They drove in silence the few blocks to the school. Again he took her hand and led her down the long hall to the kindergarten room.

The teacher came to the door.

"I think Aurora will be fine now," he told her. "I will pick her up today. Please let me know if there are any problems."

"Thank you, Rev. Justin. Come, Aurora."

He watched through the window in the door as his lovely daughter took off her coat, hung it up, and went to join the group sitting on the carpet. As he left, he ached inside. She was small and vulnerable, and there was so much for her to learn.

He glanced into the fourth grade room as he passed. Jonathan's blond head was bent over his desk as he concentrated on his reading. He wanted to stop but thought it best not to interrupt. But then Jonathan looked up and grinned. He came to the door.

"Hi, Dad. What are you doing here?"

"I brought Aurora to school."

"You did? Good. Everyone's been teasing me about my cry-baby sister. Want me to bring her home at noon?"

"No, Son. I'll come and get her. Here's a dollar. You and Gary get a treat after school."

He was rewarded with a beaming smile. "Thanks, Dad. See you."

Now, Julia was his problem. How could he handle her? As he drove home he prayed for wisdom.

He went into the living room and sank into his chair. He felt weak and tired. Grace came and climbed into his lap, cuddled down without talking, and sucked her thumb.

Julia was ignoring him, her lips pinched together and her eyes red. She ran the vacuum and stormed around cleaning unnecessarily.

Mrs. Greeley brought him a mug of coffee and the morning paper. She took Grace to tuck her in for her nap. He tried to relax.

Julia finished cleaning and stalked into the kitchen. He could hear her angry voice railing at Mrs. Greeley, but he didn't try to sort out what the words were.

He watched the clock, and when it was time he went to get Aurora. He ignored Julia's violent protests.

On the way home he asked, "Honey, were you a good girl?"

"Yes, Daddy."

"What did you do?"

She forgot herself for a bit as she told him about the day's activities.

"I'm glad you had fun."

She sobered as she looked at him and her face puckered.

"Now don't you do that. You are a big girl, and you will act like one."

She looked away.

Julia met them at the door. She was amazed as Aurora told her how much fun she had and gave her the picture she had made. Julia hung it on the bulletin board for them all to admire.

Edward knew that he still had to confront Julia. At lunch he announced that he was taking her out to dinner, just the two of them.

She protested and made excuses but finally gave in.

He chose a restaurant on the north side of San Francisco Bay. It was famous for its sea food and expensive, but he wanted everything about this evening to be special.

The drive into the city was enjoyable and relaxing. Both were trying to be pleasant and avoid unpleasant topics. Julia was excited about the unusual place he had chosen. Her friends had raved about the gourmet food served there.

Their table by the windows provided a perfect spot to watch the setting sun paint everything gold. Windows across the bay flared reflected light. As darkness came, the cities were decorated with sparkling jewels. The Bay Bridge seemed like a necklace connecting them. It was a beautiful evening.

"You look lovely tonight," he told her. Candle light softened the lines around her eyes and mouth. Her hair framed her face in graceful waves of highlighted darkness. Her dress was a flattering shade of blue, softly draped. She put her hand on the pearls at her throat, the very ones he had given her as his new bride. He knew at that moment that he still loved her deeply, and felt that the kind, loving Julia still existed in this unhappy woman.

"Julia, I enjoy being with you alone." He held her hand across the table.

"I do too, Edward. I wish we had more time."

"It isn't quite so bad now that I am at Pleasant Valley permanently. I enjoy serving one congregation. I wasn't sure at first, but I like it now. Especially since you are such a great part of it. Your music adds so much."

"I'm glad. They are nice people."

They discussed church happenings and friendly topics as their dinner was served and enjoyed. They even reminisced about their courtship days and early times together. It was so good to laugh together again.

After dessert they asked for more coffee. The waiter brought a carafe and set it on the table over a candle flame.

"Can we talk about Aurora now?" he asked.

Her face changed. "Why did you spank her so hard? You bruised her. She's delicate."

He took a deep breath. "Honey, Aurora looks small and dainty, but, thanks to your excellent care, she is very strong and healthy."

"But you hit her so hard!"

He had a sudden vision of Jonathan's battered body. Groaning inwardly, he reached and took her hand. "Don't you think she needed the spanking?"

She didn't pull her hand away. "Yes, she did. But, Edward, she's so special . . . so beautiful . . . so talented. She needs special handling."

"Granted, she is special. But, Honey, she must not be spoiled and indulged."

"You've said that so many times. I don't spoil her. Not at all."

"Are you sure?"

"Well, maybe a little."

"You must let her go."

She looked at him in alarm. "Let her go?"

"She has to grow up. Other places and people must

come into her life. She must learn to get along on her own."

"You're right. I'll find a voice teacher for her . . . the best . . . and dancing. She should have some ballet for learning gracefulness and poise, you know."

"Julia, dancing?"

"Yes, and a charm course. . . . Maybe some modeling."

"Julia, she's only a child of five."

"Just the right time to start . . . "

"Stop." He held up his hand. Then he took off his glasses, rubbed his forehead, and replaced them. "Honey, Aurora has to go to school. She has to learn to read and write. She has to learn to get along with people. Maybe, when she is much older we can consider those things. If we have the money . . . "

"Money? We must have the money. God gave us this child. He expects us to give her every chance . . . "

"God gave us Jonathan and Grace also."

"Oh, Jonathan is self-reliant. He will make it on his own."

"I have noticed that he is seldom home. Have you thought about that?"

"A boy his age is in the social group stage. He wants to be with boys his own age. He spends most of his time next door at Kimball's. He and Gary get along perfectly. Mrs. Kimball likes them there."

"I know, but why aren't they ever in our house?"

"Boys like to play rough. They're just too noisy and boisterous for Aur . . . our girls. Boys are better off being outside a great deal."

He poured more coffee. "God gave us Grace, too."

"You are the one that wanted her . . . to solve all our problems . . . "

"She is so much like you with dark hair and lovely

eyes. So cuddly and sweet." He reached to take her hand again, but she pulled away and did not smile.

"She is your daughter, and you got Mrs. Greeley to take care of her."

"And to help you."

"She does make it easier for me."

"Then why do you argue with her and order her around?"

"Edward, I think you would be glad if I took Aurora and left."

He caught his breath, almost spilling his coffee. He set it down carefully and looked straight into her eyes. "That is not true, and you know it."

"Would you ask Mrs. Greeley to leave?"

"If I thought you could handle things alone."

"That's not fair . . ."

"Honey, she has been a God-send. She has freed you to help me with church activities. She has done the heavy cleaning and taken care of the baby."

"I know."

"You want me to tell her to go?"

"Not really, I guess. I don't know what I want."

"She probably will leave on her own account. Her patience can't last forever. You are rough on her. Why don't you work it out with her to be gone more than she is? She has a home in Pleasant Valley. Maybe she would prefer to be there more, now that Grace is older. She doesn't need to live in any longer."

"I'll talk to her. Aurora's lessons will take a lot of my time. I must shop . . ."

"That is something else, Dear. Money . . . our savings are almost gone. You know that my salary is smaller than it would have been in another job, but you said you respected my decision to serve God. I need your help. We must cut back."

"How can we?"

"I'm sure if you think about it you will see some ways."

"I'll try. I do love you, Edward. Oh, it's late. I must find a phone. Aurora . . . the children. I must check on them."

"Julia, please relax."

She sank back into her chair.

"Honey, I've enjoyed this evening. We will do this often, not this fancy, but evenings together."

"We'll see. It's so hard to get away. The children need me. Let's go home." She got up abruptly, stiffened, and then leaned across the table above him, her hands flat on the table. "Don't you ever spank Aurora again. Not ever!" She turned and hurried to the door. Her mood had changed drastically, and it was frightening to see.

Edward threw his napkin on the table and followed her. He was miles down the road before he remembered he had forgotten to leave a tip.

CHAPTER VII

Easter

Easter Sunday was always special. Julia was completely at ease accompanying the congregation as they sang the Easter hymns.

Edward stood to read the Bible passages speaking of Christ's victorious resurrection. His voice was strong and resonant.

Julia noticed he was looking older. Sometimes he frowned as if he were in pain. She should insist that he have a complete check-up.

She adjusted herself on the organ bench, checking the settings for her offertory solo. The morning prayer was taking longer than usual.

She had come to love this small church. After seven years she knew each person well. Of course, today there were many guests and the church was packed. The colors from the windows danced as the sun shone through them. The scent of lilies and greens permeated the sanctuary.

Her special guest was there, sitting in a back pew. He

was wearing a bright pink shirt. She had told no one of her visit in San Francisco a month ago. She had given him a cash gift, and yet she was surprised that he had accepted her invitation. It was so exciting to have such an important person in the service.

She looked over her family, a usual Sunday morning ritual. Aurora sat in the choir looking more angelic than usual. Jonathan, now fifteen, was sitting in the balcony with Gary Kimball and the other boys his age. He insisted on being called "Jon" . . . it hardly seemed possible that he was growing up, becoming quite independent. All the boys had a guarded, closed look of assumed boredom. Jon was going to be quite handsome when he outgrew this awkward age.

Grace sat beside Mrs. Greeley. At seven she was a happy, well adjusted child. She looked quite pretty in the fluffy pink dress handed down from Aurora. Mrs. Greeley's visiting family filled the rest of the pew. Julia, although she wouldn't admit it, missed having her live with them. She had moved out when Grace started school, but they saw her often, and she still came to help them out when they needed her.

The prayer was over. Julia became absorbed as she played a masterful and intricate solo using the full range of the organ. Then she let the music die away to a series of low single notes introducing Aurora's song.

How beautiful she was standing in a beam of light in her white choir robe! Her silver curls were piled high and held by a crimson ribbon. Her eyes were downcast, her hands folded. Julia's heart almost burst with pride as she started to sing "The Holy City." The difficulty of the song disappeared as the pure clear tones of the child's voice mastered them. Julia was so moved by the last series of hosannas that she was tempted to stop playing the organ and just listen.

There was complete silence as she sat down. Slowly Edward stood up to continue the service. Julia noticed the glow on his face as several people wiped their eyes. It had been perfect. She was sure that her special guest had been impressed.

When the service ended, Julia went to stand with Edward and greet people as they filed out. Many praised Aurora's solo; several mentioned how much they appreciated Julia's contribution as a musician, and some even mentioned Edward's message.

The crowd thinned. Julia met the man in the pink shirt as he came to them.

"Edward, this is Albert Viert, one of the world's foremost voice teachers. I invited him to come and hear Aurora."

Albert Viert's hair formed a halo of white around a bald spot. His eyes were kind, yet stern. His nose was bulbous, his lips thin. The vivid pink shirt he wore contrasted with his dark suit.

"Reverend, the service was inspiring."

"The music?" Julia inquired.

"Good, yes, good for a small church. Your daughter sings well. You say she is ten years old? Amazing! Yes."

"You could give her lessons?" Julia asked, looking anxiously into his face.

"I take no new students, especially no children. But this little one . . . I could consider."

"Wait, Mr. Viert." Edward held up his hand. "Aurora is still a child. Her voice is far from mature, and we cannot afford expensive lessons."

"Reverend Justin, I know this, and I would agree she is too young, but, her voice . . . yes, she should begin. Just easy things for now. Maybe once or twice a month. No more. Could this be?" He turned to Julia. "You bring her to me. Next Friday. Two P.M. We shall see."

He held out his card and turned to leave. There was a man waiting for him by a car at the curb.

Julia glowed with happiness. She took Edward's arm and squeezed it.

Jon ambled up. "Hey, Mom, I'm going to Kimball's for dinner. Be home sometime."

"Jon, wait," she called.

He jumped over the door into a disreputable old convertible crowded with noisy teenagers. It roared away leaving a cloud of fumes.

Grace came to stand beside her dad. She slid her hand into his, and he squeezed it. Aurora joined them, frowning.

"Let's go home. I'm starving."

Julia was still floating with excitement over Mr. Viert's visit when Edward showed up unexpectedly for lunch on Wednesday. All week she had talked of nothing but how great Albert Viert was. How amazing that he would consider teaching such a young child!

It seemed that at least a dozen times she had changed her plans of what Aurora should wear to the Friday appointment with the voice teacher. Edward had laid down the law . . . they would buy nothing new.

Julia flitted around fixing a sandwich for him and heating a can of soup.

She would not listen as he tried to caution her about getting overly excited. He told her again to calm down—that they could not afford expensive lessons. He had wanted her to go visiting with him this afternoon, but he saw it was no use.

As soon as he left, Julia dropped everything and went to the piano. Great peals of praise poured from her fingers on the keyboard, crashing chords, surging melodies.

The phone was ringing. The discord finally shook her out of her ecstasy.

"Mrs. Justin, this is the secretary calling from school. There has been an accident . . . no, nothing alarming. Would you please bring a change of clothing for Aurora? I assure you . . ."

Time blurred. She couldn't find her keys. She frantically dumped everything out of her black leather bag. There they were—at the bottom. She grabbed a small suitcase and shoved in an armload of Aurora's things. The car wouldn't start . . . not when it was in neutral. "Calm down," she scolded herself. "You must be strong. Whatever it is . . ."

She slammed to a stop in the no parking area, in front of the school, grabbed the suitcase, and ran to the office.

"Mrs. Justin. In here."

The secretary took her into the nurse's room. Aurora lay on the cot, pale and crying. There were angry red scratches across her face and her bare arms showed more scratches and bruises already turning dark.

"Baby, what is it? What happened?"

"Momma! I want to go home."

"You shall. At once."

"Mrs. Justin, I'll help her dress. The principal and her teacher want to talk to you. Just go in there."

"No, I must get her to a doctor. Call an ambulance."

"The nurse has checked her. She will be fine. Please, Mrs. Justin." The woman took her arm and propelled her into the other room and then into the office.

Mr. Blane closed the door behind her and led her to a chair. Mrs. Wainwright, Aurora's teacher, was sitting looking at her soberly.

"Tell me at once what happened? I must get her to a doctor," she demanded.

Mr. Blane sat behind his desk. "Mrs. Justin, Aurora was in a fight."

"A fight? A fight?"

"You see," Mrs. Wainwright continued, "I insisted that Aurora go out for noon recess. It is a lovely day. She prefers to stay inside and is a helpful child. Many of the teachers give her tasks to do. She is very well-adjusted with adults and is a sweet lovely child."

"A fight?"

Mr. Blane cleared his throat. "She does not get along well with other children."

"I don't understand."

"I have tried to tell you about this at conference times, Mrs. Justin." Mrs. Wainwright went to stand by the window. "Aurora reads and writes beautifully. She studies and does her assignments flawlessly. But . . . but . . ."

"Yes?"

"Aurora is too sweet, too beautiful. Yes, and too spoiled. She won't be crossed and insists on her own way."

Julia sat in horrified silence.

"You dress her like a frilly little doll in spotless clothes with lace and ruffles. She is too sweet, prissy, and completely unbearable to the children. She insists on flaunting herself and her talents. They can't stand it and tease her unmercifully, so she makes every excuse to stay away from them. But today I made her go outside."

"One thing led to another," Mr. Blane added. "We have a group of girls that are from a tougher part of town. They followed her around mimicking her; then they began to push her. Aurora pulled away from their dirty hands. Someone tore her dress. She hit back. Before the duty teacher could get there it was a full scale fight with Aurora on the bottom of the heap. She got scratched, bruised and dirty. Otherwise, only her dignity is hurt."

Julia could contain herself no longer. Jumping to her feet, eyes blazing, she let loose an angry tirade that was interrupted only by her daughter at the door.

"Momma, I want to go home." She was dressed in clothes that didn't match and there were tears on her face.

"Yes, Baby, at once. Come." They went to the car, and Julia drove straight to the emergency door of the hospital. A nurse took Aurora away down the hall.

Julia paced up and down, her thoughts in complete turmoil.

The doctor came to her, holding Aurora by the hand. "Mrs. Justin, your daughter is fine. A few bruises and scratches. Otherwise . . ."

"Those scratches are on her face! She'll be scarred. Her beautiful face!!"

"No, Mrs. Justin. Here is a prescription for some salve. You follow the directions, and there will be no trace in a few days. Now, take her home. Mrs. Justin, you take two of those tablets I prescribed for you, or you will be sick. Do you understand?"

"Yes, yes. My poor baby!"

"Oh, Mom, stop it! I'm okay. You should see the other girls. I bit one of them!"

They drove home, and Aurora began to laugh as she told the details of her adventure.

"Bet we all get it at school. That was some fight!"

"You are never going back there again."

"Oh, Mom, don't be silly. Boy, are those girls in trouble! Nobody will dare to touch me again."

"But, Honey, those scratches . . ."

"I know." She admired them in the mirror on the

visor. "Won't everyone be sorry for me? I can't wait for Jon to see. Boy, will he laugh!"

"Your father will be horrified. He will want to sue . . ."

"Oh, Mom, you're crazy. He wants me to be tough and fight back. You see. He will be proud of me."

"Now, Baby, you calm down. I'll have you tucked in bed soon and get some warm cocoa . . ."

"Stop it, Mom. I'll put you to bed. You need it more than I. Wow, did you ever tell off Mr. Blane and Miss Wainwright!"

"I don't even remember what I said."

"I hope they don't remember! Guess I'll stay home tomorrow."

"Friday is your first lesson and you look terrible."

"Old man Viert won't care how I look. He just wants to hear my gorgeous voice."

"Aurora . . ."

"I'll stay home Friday, too. By Monday these bruises should look neat . . . all black and blue and green and yellow . . ."

CHAPTER VIII

Drunk

Grace sat on the back steps watching Jon and Gary working on their car. It was an old, blue Oldsmobile sedan loaded with chrome, waxed and polished to perfection.

The motor sputtered into life and collapsed with an asthmatic cough. The boys ducked their heads under the hood again.

"Hey, Grace," Jon called standing up and stretching. "How about getting us some lemonade? We're boiling."

"Will you give me a ride?"

"Sure . . . sure."

She went inside and fixed a tray. Mom and Rora were practicing as usual. How could they stick at it like that on a beautiful, hot Saturday in May?

Maybe Jon and Gary would take her swimming with them this afternoon.

She took the tray out, and they sprawled on the lawn under a tree and drank lemonade and munched cookies.

"Aurora sings great for a kid of twelve," Gary commented.

"Yeah," Jon muttered.

"She's pretty, too."

"Oh, for Pete's sake . . ."

Grace rolled flat on her back and looked up through the leaves to the blue sky. Little streams of sunlight got in her eyes. She put her arm over them.

"Hey, Jon, think we can get the car going in time? The party should be a blast. Stan said he was getting a whole case of . . ."

"Shut up, Gary. Come on. Let's get to work. I've got an idea about what is wrong with the car. Thanks, Grace."

She ignored them. There was an ant crawling up her arm, and it tickled exquisitely. Exquisitely, she liked that word.

The music stopped. Aurora came out the back door and went over to the car.

Grace leaned up on one arm. Even on a Saturday, Aurora dressed up. Her pants were apple green. Her blouse was a very pale pink and a matching scarf tied back her long curly hair. Sickening. She stuck out her chest, and you could see her bra. Disgusting!

"Hi," she trilled. "How's it going?"

"Almost have it," Gary answered. "You look neat, Rora."

"Thanks. I get to go with you, don't I, Jon?"

"No way."

"Oh, come on. You want me, Gary. Don't you?"

"This is a party for big kids," Jon said. "You're not even a teen-ager yet."

"I look like one though. Don't I, Gary?" She put her hand on his arm.

Grace rolled over on her stomach in disgust.

"Rora, Honey, you look good to me," Gary said putting his arm around her.

"Cut it out!" Jon said. "Hey, Gary, grab this wire. We'll solder it here. Bet that will do it."

Aurora came to sit gracefully beside Grace on the lawn. "Gary is cute, isn't he?"

"Oh, puke!"

"You're awful," she giggled. "Wow, it's hot."

"Let's go swimming. We could ride our bikes."

"Good idea. Mom wouldn't like it though. I have to sing tomorrow, and she doesn't want me to overdo."

"Oh, baloney. One dumb song in church. Besides, you never swim much. You just lie in the sun and try to look beautiful."

"I don't have to try. I am. Too bad you are so ugly."

"I am not." She sat up. "Just ask Daddy."

"Daddy is prejudiced."

The car roared into life, and the motor ran smoothly. Jon and Gary yelled and jumped into the car. Before the girls could reach them, the car zoomed out of the driveway leaving a cloud of oily smoke.

"Oh, rats," Aurora muttered.

"Let's go to the park. I'm going swimming. Coming?"

"No. Too hot. I've got a neat book, a romance. I'm going to read in the hammock."

"Hey, Rora, do you really like all that music and singing?" Grace asked her sister.

"Of course, Dummy."

"I mean, really."

"Well . . . I don't like to practice all the time, and I don't like Mom trying to run every minute of my life. But I do like having people tell me how good my voice is and how beautiful I am."

"Disgusting."

"Oh, oh, little sister. You are jealous."

"Oh no, I'm not. I just can't understand how you can be so different when you are with us kids and so sweet and lovely and adorable and precious with grown-ups!"

"Hey, it's a skill I have developed. I get what I want that way."

"What do you want, Rora?"

"Fame. Riches. The whole world. You just watch me, Gracie. I'm going to get it." She jumped up and danced into the house.

Grace sat still hugging her knees. Those things were wrong to want. You were supposed to want God and His love above everything else and to love others. Daddy told about it in his sermons.

That was what she was going to do. Put Jesus Christ first.

She got up and went to the kitchen and made herself a fat peanut butter and mayonnaise sandwich. She wrapped it and put it with an apple in a sack.

"Going to the park, Mom," she called.

"Okay, Sweety. Be home by five," Julia answered. She was still practicing on the piano.

That night Grace couldn't get to sleep. Her sunburn made it too hot to cover up, but if she didn't, she chilled. She wanted a drink.

There was a light downstairs. She tiptoed. Daddy was asleep in his chair, papers spilled at his feet. She kneeled down to pick them up.

"Hi, Honey," he said covering a yawn. He stretched his arms high and then groaned as a pain caught him. He doubled over.

"Daddy, are you all right?"

"Sure, Honey. Just a stitch."

She noticed sweat on his forehead. "What did the doctor say?"

"I didn't see him. He was out."

"Bet you didn't try very hard."

He laughed and touched her arm. She winced away. "Oh, oh. Sunburn."

"Yes. I always forget the first swim of the season, and get burned."

"Get the lotion; I'll put it on for you. Is that why you couldn't sleep?"

They went into the kitchen, and he gently applied the soothing lotion. Their companionship was a warm, close, and loving one. Grace fixed them a snack.

"You didn't tell me why you were still up," she said.

"Guess I didn't. I wanted to go over my sermon for tomorrow, and Jonathan isn't home yet."

"It's only 12:30. He and Gary were going to a party."

"I know. At seventeen he doesn't need anyone to wait up for him. I just felt anxious for some reason. He is a good kid, isn't he, Grace?"

"He's good to me."

"I know. Why did you say it that way?"

"I don't like to say, Daddy."

"Tell me, please."

"I don't know anything bad, Daddy. I just hear them talk."

"What did they say?"

"Gary said the party should be a blast. Someone was getting a case of . . ."

"Case of what?"

"Jon made him shut up."

"I was afraid he was getting into that. I have suspected it for some time. I just hoped it was natural for him to make excuses not to do things with me now that he is older. He doesn't want to go to games, or play golf, or bowl. It's been quite a while since we have done anything together. He seems to avoid me sometimes."

"Don't feel bad. He wants to be with the guys and the girls. He likes Nancy real well, and she's cute. I like her."

"Nancy Tyler? She is cute. Nice family, too. Is it serious?"

"Could be. Jon will be okay, Daddy. He's a good car mechanic."

"I hoped he would go on to college . . ."

"Hey, Daddy, would you teach me to bowl?"

"Sure, Honey. I'd like that. We'll go next week."

"Are you going to the doctor first?"

"Now, Grace . . ."

"I mean it, Daddy. I worry about you."

"You do?"

"Yes. I'm afraid for you."

"Okay. I'll make an appointment Monday. How is the sunburn? Think you can sleep?"

A car drove into the driveway. They heard Gary's voice and a door slam. They waited.

After several minutes Edward stood. "Something must be wrong." He switched on the outside light as he went out the back door. Grace followed.

Gary must have gone on home. Jon sat hunched over on the passenger side. As the car door was pulled open, he sagged out into Edward's arms. He smelled horrible. There was vomit down the front of his jacket. His breath was rancid. He was out, cold drunk.

"Oh, Daddy . . ."

"You'll have to help me with him."

Edward shook Jon and finally managed to get him to come alive enough to walk between them into the kitchen. They didn't dare stop. It took all their combined strength to get him up the stairs to his room. He collapsed across the bed.

Edward stood weaving, his face pale, and gasping for breath. Grace made him sit down, and he hung his head between his knees.

Julia came to the door and stood horrified. She sunk to her knees beside the bed. "He's drunk. How awful!"

Edward raised his head. "Now stop that, Julia. Help me get him to bed."

"I can't touch him."

"Ooo, does he stink!" Aurora came to stand over them. Her filmy nightgown floated around her.

Grace was gently wiping off Jon's face. Edward tried to get his smelly jacket off.

"You're getting everything on the bed filthy," Julia said.

Edward stood up and took command. "Aurora and Grace, you get to bed. Julia, if you can be helpful and sensible, you stay. Otherwise, you go too."

She stood a moment and then pushed the girls out of the room and shut the door firmly.

Aurora was giggling. "Jon will get it this time. Wow!"

"You are so repulsive."

"Look who's talking. You're going to have to take a shower to get rid of that smell. Oh, yuck!"

"You sure didn't get yourself wrinkled."

"I never do. Good night. Pleasant dreams." She floated into her room and closed the door gently in Grace's face.

The phone rang. Grace ran down stairs to answer it.

"Justin residence? May I speak to Rev. Justin? This is Deputy Simson, Police Department."

Grace called her father to the phone and stood beside him as he answered.

"Yes? . . . A wreck? . . . Nancy Tyler . . . I'll come at once."

"What is it, Daddy?"

"Jon had a fight with Nancy, it seems. She went off with a car load of drunk kids. There was a wreck. She's hurt. One of the kids is dead. The driver is in jail. Nancy's folks asked for me."

"Oh, Daddy . . ."

"Gracie—I hate to ask you, but I'm afraid your mother would get too upset . . . can you handle this end for me? Jon's in bed and will sleep all night. When he wakes up, make sure that he eats something. Then tell him about Nancy. Will you call Gary in the morning too?

"Yes, Daddy. Are you okay?"

"I'll be fine. I love you, Grace."

"I know, Daddy."

The little girl gave her father a hug. He felt a big lump come to his throat as he kissed her cheek. He thought about the big responsibilities Grace so often handled . . . responsibilities that were really Julia's.

CHAPTER IX
Operation

"Aurora, you have been asked to sing at the Chamber of Commerce annual banquet," Julia announced returning to her place at the dinner table. "I accepted, of course. Two numbers. . . thirty dollars. Not bad, huh?"

"Do I get a new dress?"

"No way," Edward said, pouring more coffee. "That money goes to Albert Viert. We still owe him."

"Oh, Daddy, you're a tightwad."

"Sure am, Princess. Wasn't it last week you. . ."

"Grace, how about you accompanying her this time?"

"Aw, Mom. ."

"You make a beautiful team. If you practice, you could do it. I would be so proud."

"Do I have to?"

"I don't want her," Aurora said.

"Why not?" Edward asked.

Grace just smiled.

"She's a show off." Rora snapped.

"Explain, please."

"Forget it, Daddy. I don't want to play for her," Grace said.

"Aurora, explain your attitude."

"At the youth meeting after church last Sunday they asked me to sing. Grace played for me. Then she got to clowning around. Everyone egged her on. She really showed off."

Grace got up to leave the table.

"Sit down, Grace. Explain, Aurora."

"Oh, she got to playing jazz and rock, anything they asked for. It was odious."

Julia said, "I didn't know she could do that."

Grace half-stood. "Yeah, she didn't like it because the kids didn't ask her to sing any more. They just wanted me to play. I've made up my mind, no more sister acts. I'll never accompany her again."

"Sit down, Grace. Finish your meal!" Edward ordered. "You do not have to play for her again."

"I'd rather have you anyway, Mom," Aurora said.

Julia smiled. "Oh, all right, Honey." She got up to clear the table and bring dessert.

"Any word from Jon?" Edward asked.

There was silence.

"Daddy, you ask that every meal," Aurora said. "He's okay."

"I hope so. I would like to hear from him."

"Mrs. Kimball had a letter from Gary yesterday," Julia reported. "The boys have jobs in Montana on a ranch. Wonder why Jon doesn't write."

"It's obvious, Mom. You told him to go."

"Aurora, that's not so."

"Oh, yes it is. He didn't have a job after he graduated, and you told him to quit lying around. He got in your way. You got mad at him. I heard."

"Julia, is that true?" Edward asked.

"I heard it, too," Grace added.

"Julia?"

"Well." She stood holding a load of dirty dishes. "We did have words. I told him to go get a job."

"That's putting it mildly," Aurora muttered.

"So that's why he left so suddenly without telling me." Edward rubbed his forehead.

"Did he have any money?"

"I gave him some," Grace said.

"What a dummy," Aurora laughed. "You'll never see any of it again."

"I already have. He sent it back last week. But he didn't write anything but 'thanks.' "

"Your turn to wash dishes, Grace." Aurora got up and stretched languidly. "I better go practice. What shall I sing, Mom?"

"Aurora, I always wash."

"You should. I have to keep my hands nice, don't I, Mother?"

"Yes, Dear. You don't really mind, do you Grace?"

Grace didn't answer, but her face showed resignation.

Edward reached and took Grace's hand. "You wash up, Honey. I'll help, then we'll go for a ride, okay?"

No one noticed when they slipped out the back door a half-hour later and drove off into the evening. The sunset promised to be spectacular as they raced to a spot high above the valley for a good view. They sat in silence, watching the changing patterns of vivid color painted in the heavens. As the shades finally faded to pale pink and then gray, an immense harvest moon edged up over bare hills.

"It's so beautiful, Daddy."

"Can't beat God as an artist."

They sat longer in silence. Then Edward began,
"Say, Gracie, what is this about you playing the
piano so well?"

"I've been playing for ages. It just comes natural for
me. I've had lessons since I was six."

"Six?"

"Mrs. Greeley heard me playing around when Mom
and Rora were gone. She helped me and got a teacher
for me. Mrs. Bannister. . . know her?"

"Of course. She plays for the biggest church in
town."

"She's great, Daddy. She understands. I didn't want
to compete with Rora, so I practice when no one is
around, or at school. They let me use the school piano. I
just couldn't help it. Only Jon knows, and he helped me,
too."

"Honey, that costs money."

"Mrs. Greeley paid it, even when she moved away.
She said it was our secret. She didn't want you to
know."

"I owe her for that, too. . . Will you play for me?"

"Any time, Daddy. I'm sorry I didn't tell you."

"You keep a lot of things from me." His head was
hurting . . . and his stomach.

"Sorry, Dad, I just don't like to cause more trouble."

"We do seem to have plenty. . ." He leaned back,
taking off his glasses.

"Daddy, are you okay?"

"You ask me that often, Love."

"I watch you."

"Honey, I have to tell you I have to have an operation on my stomach."

"Oh, Daddy . . . "

"They say it should be simple, no problem."

"You're worried?"

"About several things. I shouldn't bother you with all of it though."

"Yes, you should, Daddy. Please tell me. I want to help."

"Your Mother. . ."

"I know, Daddy. She loves us, but, well, other things are more important to her."

"You are wise, little one. She isn't too well."

"She does get too excited and mad at times."

"Grace, has she ever. . . ever hit you?"

"No, Daddy. She has spanked me, very hard, but not for a long time."

"You didn't tell me."

"It was okay, and I learned not to ever cross her or Aurora. I just do what they say. I'm okay—honest!"

He rubbed his forehead and put his glasses back on. "Did she really send Jon away?"

"He was going anyway, Daddy. Mom wouldn't let him alone. She made him take Rora every place with him, even to parties. Rora just made trouble, so he didn't get invited any more. He would sneak out and go down to the Moonlight Tavern. . ."

"Honey, why didn't you tell me?"

"It wouldn't do any good. Gary and I finally talked him into leaving and seeing the country. They're okay, Daddy. I'm sure. Gary is a neat guy."

"But Jon didn't come to me. . ."

"He was going to. Then Mom got mad at him, and he just took off."

"Do you know where he is? I would like to write to him and send him. . . some. . . money. . ."

Grace leaned over and put her hand on his arm. "It's

okay, Daddy. They have good jobs. They got them at a
ranch. They like it. It's good for them. He'll write."

"I wish. . . I wish. . . Oh, God." He bowed his head
on the steering wheel.

"When, Daddy?"

He raised up and shook his head. "When?"

"The operation?"

"Next week. Tuesday morning."

"Does Mom know?"

"No. I just found out today."

"She'll have a fit."

"I know. I tried to avoid it, but the doctor says I
can't."

"It scares you?"

"Not really. I'll be fine, I know, but I guess this on
top of worrying about your mom and Aurora. . . She
will be out of high school next year. Then your mother is
talking of New York. . . and Paris. . . and Hollywood. . ." He hit the steering wheel with his hand.

"She'll probably get married."

"What?"

"You should see her with the guys. It's sickening."

"Oh, no. . ."

"She fools every grown up with her sugar sweetness,
but the girls all hate her because all the guys think she is
something else! She knows how to get what she wants
from everyone, even you and me. You should see how
she bribes Jon and me not to tell on her."

He groaned aloud.

"Daddy, let's go see Mrs. Greeley. I haven't seen her
except in church for months."

He started the car and drove back down the winding
road in the moonlight. The ache inside him had ba-
looned into searing pain. He drove very carefully, fight-
ing nausea and dizziness.

They were on level ground. He fumbled in his pocket. The car slowed to a stop. He took two pills, choking as he swallowed them without water.

He soothed Grace's alarm. "I'll be okay. Just give me a few minutes." His vision cleared, and he drove on slowly.

"Turn left here, Daddy."

He followed her directions until she told him to stop. She jumped out and returned with Mrs. Greeley. They both helped him into the house.

Soon he felt much better. They made him stretch out on the couch, and Mrs. Greeley called the doctor. He ordered them to go to the hospital immediately. Surgery was rescheduled for the next morning.

Mrs. Greeley insisted that Grace stay overnight with her. After they drove Edward to the hospital, they returned to Mrs. Greeley's house, and she called Julia. Immediately upset, Julia insisted on going straight to the hospital.

Mrs. Greeley tucked Grace lovingly into a sleeping bag on the couch, and knelt beside her.

"Can you sleep, Gracie?"

"Daddy was so worried. . ."

"About what, Dear? The operation?"

"Not so much about that as about Jon and Rora and money. He was mad at me because I don't tell him things. He found out about our music secret. Rora got jealous and told."

"That's all right. I'm sure he's proud of you and surprised. I know he won't be mad at you."

"Well, not mad, but sad. Like it was too much. Lessons and clothes and trips. . ."

"I think we had better pray, don't you? Seems like we need God especially right now."

They each prayed, and Grace drifted off to sleep

knowing everything was going to be okay.

Late the next day the doctors assured them that Rev. Justin had come through remarkably well and would soon recover. He would have some diet and activity restrictions, but otherwise he would recover fully.

When they let Grace go in to see him, Julia left them alone. Grace sat on a stool beside the bed and held his hand. "You're okay, Daddy?"

"There you go again, asking me that question."

"I know. It's so good to see you. I've been so worried. I prayed a lot."

"No more worry, Honey." He reached to touch her hair. "Is everything at home all right?"

"Mom's been great. I guess she got scared, Daddy. She even telephoned Jon and told him. She asked him to come home. Oh, I wasn't supposed to tell you. It's a surprise."

He laughed. "I'll be surprised, I promise. It's so good to see you."

"I'm so glad you're okay, Daddy," Grace leaned over to kiss his forehead.

CHAPTER X
Family

Edward glanced at his watch. It was 5:30. He enjoyed sitting in the lounge chair on the front porch, and several friends had stopped by. Now he was tired, and gnawing pains told him he should eat. In fact, food was overdue. He must go get something. Yet he knew that weak feeling would attack him when he got up, and he hesitated.

Aurora had promised to come home to fix dinner. Her practice with some of the school band members should have been over long ago. Her tennis lesson should have been over, too.

"Hi, Dad," Jon called as he drove up. He leaped over the door of his ancient rebuilt red sports car and came to sit on the top step. "How you doing?"

"Not bad, Jon. Didn't expect you home today."

"Got hungry. Gary is cooking tonight, and I'm tired of canned spaghetti. Besides, I need some clothes washed. Is Grace around?"

"How is the apartment working out?"

"Good, Dad. The four of us get along great. My boss says I'm getting to be a fantastic mechanic, and he wants me to go into the apprentice program. He'll set it up."

"Is that what you want? Remember, you have acceptances from two colleges."

"Not sure . . . Gary wants me to go to junior college with him."

"You should decide soon."

"Yeah. What's for dinner?"

"Seems like we are on our own. Aurora was supposed to be home by now."

"Where are Grace and Mom?"

"I insisted that Mom take Grace to San Francisco and get her some new clothes. She has worn Rora's cast-offs long enough. She doesn't even look good in the same styles."

"Good going, Dad! You know, Grace is a good-looking chick. The guys like her because she's not on the make. She's a good kid. How come Rora didn't insist on going?"

"I wouldn't let her."

"That must have been a scene!"

"There are times when my wishes get followed," Edward said, only half-joking. "Let's go find something to eat."

He got up too fast, and the dizziness caused him to stagger. Jon caught his arm, and the feeling passed immediately.

"Take it easy, Pops."

"I'm okay. It's to be expected so soon after surgery, but I am getting stronger. I plan to work some next week." He sank into a kitchen chair.

"Just don't push it too fast." Jon's voice was muffled, his head in the refrigerator. "There's some cold beef here, and some soup. We'll have something to eat in no time."

Jon set things on the table, and they discussed the latest sports events as they ate. Then they became absorbed in discussing mechanics.

Edward had always been interested in engines and had almost done what Jon was considering. His mother had made him promise to try one year of college, and as she expected, he was hooked. Once in a while, at odd moments, he wondered how different his life would have been if he had become a mechanic, or married a less demanding woman.

This added to his dilemma about Jon. Should he insist that his son go to college? He could afford to help him now. They had discussed it several times.

"Another cup of coffee, Dad?"

"Please, Son."

The back door slammed, and Aurora ran in. Her very short white tennis dress looked lovely on her. She stopped and put her hand over her mouth.

"Oh my, I forgot. Sorry, Dad."

"Up to your old tricks, Rora." Jon stood facing her. "You know Dad needs to eat at regular times."

"It's late." She glanced at her watch. "I have to change. We're going to a concert."

"Aurora," Jon said taking her arm. "Dad isn't well yet. You promised to be home two hours ago."

"I got held up." She pouted and shrugged off his hand.

"You're mad because Dad wouldn't let you go with Mom and Grace."

"Oh, hush." She went to stand behind Edward's chair and put her arms around him. "Daddy is just fine." She kissed the bald spot on his head. "I really have to change. Georgie will be back for me in forty minutes. There's a concert."

"Georgie? George Fields. Oh sure, George hasn't been to a concert in his whole life. Oh, a tavern concert, maybe."

"Jon, you shut up!"

"Aurora, do I know George Fields?" Edward asked.

She sat gracefully on the kitchen stool and reached for a piece of meat. She munched it daintily, picking it apart a bit at a time with her fingers.

"Sure, Dad. He plays football at Cal. State. He's big and hunky and gorgeous."

"Little old for you, isn't he?"

Jon slammed his coffee mug down. "You bet he is. He hangs out with that crowd at Jenny's Place down by the free-way. It even has topless dancers. . ."

"You shut up. You are always shooting off your mouth. . ."

"I care about you."

"Like hell you do. . ."

"Aurora! Jon! Stop that at once. Aurora, you are not leaving this house tonight. And don't you ever talk like that again!"

"Oh, Dad, come off it." She stood up, hands on her hips. "I'll do just as I please. I'm too big for you to spank and . . . and besides, you're not even man enough to keep Mom at home." She sauntered insolently through the swinging door.

"I could beat her. . ." Jon choked, half standing, livid with rage.

"No, Son." Edward bowed his head, feeling his weakness. A blackness engulfed him momentarily.

Jon came to him and helped him from the kitchen to

the living room couch. He covered him gently with a bright afghan.

The front doorbell rang. Jon went to see who was there. The Tylers stood at the door.

Mr. Tyler asked, "May we see Rev. Justin just for a minute? Nancy is in town for a few days and wanted to stop by."

"Come in."

The Tylers were pleasant-looking people, open and friendly. They insisted that Edward stay on the couch, and brought chairs near him. Mrs. Tyler handed Jon a box of cookies. They talked quietly.

Edward was genuinely glad to see them. They attended his church, and both were strong leaders.

Nancy was a lovely, dark-haired, dark-eyed girl, small and neat. "Pastor, I will never be able to thank you enough for your help the night of my accident," she told Edward.

"It was a pleasure to be there and hold the hand of one of my favorite people. That was quite a few years ago."

"I won't ever forget. It was a turning point in my life."

"How is school?"

"You know, I really like it. I didn't think I would. There are a lot of neat people." She looked over at Jon and smiled.

"I'll bet there are," he returned her smile. He came to sit on the arm of the couch. "You are looking great, as always."

"Why, thank you, Jon."

They all laughed. Edward noticed that Jon's interest in Nancy seemed to have endured, even though they had not seen each other for quite a while. The time passed too quickly, and the Tylers got up to leave.

"Dad, can you spare me?" Jon whispered.

"You bet, Son. Good luck."

Jon left with the Tylers. Edward sank back onto the pillows, closing his eyes. He felt extremely tired.

Yet, there was a satisfied feeling. Jon was going to make it. Since he had returned, they had spent quite a bit of time together. They had been candid and open with each other. Understanding had been added to their love. Jon was attending church again, and Edward was pleased to see how he had matured.

But Aurora? He put his arm over his face. The house was silent. There was no movement. She was gone. She had sneaked out.

How could he feel so totally inadequate? Before the surgery, he had known the desperation of hoping that his time had come so that God would take him away from all these insurmountable problems. He had ached for release, but it was not to be. God had left him here. These were still his problems.

Yet, God had renewed his faith in His strength. Weakly he once more prayed for each member of his family. If only he could be more in command, more capable. . . .

He reached far back in his memory to recall his lovely young bride. How many years had gone by? Jon was twenty-two. He and Julia had been married twenty-three years. It would soon be a quarter of a century. Good years. . .bad years. . . .

Always when his mind wandered he would inevitably see Jonathan's battered bruised swollen face, and the pain would grip him again. Now the pain was muted and bittersweet. Jon was a man. He had escaped the hurt of those days and was responsible for his own choices.

Edward prayed that they would be the right ones.

He shifted his position on the couch, raising his knees. Reaching to readjust his afghan was an effort. He sank back, but thoughts of Aurora would not go away.

Aurora. He had to think and pray for her. It was almost impossible to realize that such a beautiful creature had resulted from his love and union with Julia. She was so lovely, with that unusual, almost white curling hair, those immense changeable blue-green eyes, the perfect features, generous lips, and those dimples. At seventeen her body was exquisite and provocative in the eyes of every man who looked at her, he was sure. When she sang, she used her voice as a rare and priceless instrument, charming her listeners to the utmost emotional response. She was learning her power as a performer and as a woman, but she was too young and inexperienced to know the restraints such talent and beauty must impose.

"Oh, God," he prayed, "how can I get through to her? Is it too late?" He felt he should try at least once more, but was afraid she didn't respect him and wouldn't listen.

Then he allowed himself to think of Grace. As always, peace seemed to come with her name. She was everything he had desired in a child—obedient, self-reliant, sympathic, loving. She loved people, and people loved her because she was open, thoughtful, and caring. At fifteen her gift of music was evident, but her primary gift was love. She had not been spoiled by exploitation.

Julia and Aurora were blind to the good in her and heckled her constantly. Grace had learned at a young age how to handle unfair criticism. She just let it go by her and didn't strike back. Edward knew he could never repay Mrs. Greeley for her help in rearing Grace. It was a debt he would always owe.

Grace was beautiful, too. Her hair was a lustrous brown. Her eyes were large and clear blue. The sprinkling of freckles over her upturned nose and laughing mouth made her irresistible. At fifteen she held promise of slim, tall, poised maturity. Any man who could look past Aurora for a moment would be held by Grace's lasting, serene presence.

Grace was a true gift from God. She was the one who needed his protection. The others could go their own ways, and they would. Edward would see that Grace was provided for, that Julia and Aurora would not leave her penniless and wanting. They would if they found out about some money he had inherited. Grace deserved an education and the opportunity to develop her ability to serve and give. He would see his attorney soon and get it all settled.

The lamp at his head was turned on suddenly.

"Daddy." Grace bent to kiss him. "You should be in bed."

"Oh, you're back. I must have dozed off." He struggled to sit up.

"Well, Edward, you're still up." Julia sank into a chair. She dumped her armload of packages on the floor and kicked off her shoes. "Am I tired!"

"Daddy, have you had supper?"

"Where is Aurora?" Julia asked.

"Jon fixed dinner for us. Aurora is out."

"Jon? Hey, that's neat. What happened to Rora?"

"She came in about seven and left almost immediately."

"Where did she go?" Julia asked. "She was supposed to practice tonight."

"Out. She said something about a concert. Did you get some nice things, Grace?"

"Oh yes, Daddy. Wait until you see. It was such fun!" She talked on, dragging colorful clothing from packages and dancing around with them. He had never seen her quite like this, and his throat swelled with a tight feeling.

"Look at this, Daddy. A bathing suit!"

"Those two tiny pieces of orange cloth?"

"Uh huh. I'll model all my stuff for you. Thank you, Daddy. I love you, love you." She almost smothered him in a big hug. Her hair tickled his nose.

"I'll fix us a snack," Julia said. She went to the kitchen in her stocking feet. Edward wondered how she stayed so thin with all the extra snacks she had.

"I'll help, Mom, after I pick up all this stuff. You stay here, Daddy. I'll bring you something."

When Julia and Grace went up to bed, he insisted on staying on the couch. He felt it vital to talk to Aurora. Grace had made him comfortable with his pillow and a blanket. He slept.

If Aurora hadn't stumbled over a chair in the dining room, she wouldn't have awakened him.

"Aurora?"

"Oh no, Daddy? Are you still up?" She stayed in the darkness by the stairs.

"Come here."

"Oh, come off it, Daddy. I'm bushed. Let's talk tomorrow."

"Come here." He swung his feet to the floor and sat up. His watch said 3:30. She came and sat on the hearthstone out of the circle of light from the lamp turned low at the far side of the room. Her face was a white blur in the semi-darkness.

He prayed for the right words. "Princess, I don't like to see you tire yourself with such late hours."

Her giggle was unpleasant.

Wrong approach. "Honey, I. . ."

"Okay, Dad. I'll say it for you. You and Mom have told me over and over. I'm too young. I'm special. Got to take care of my voice. All that stuff."

"It's true, Honey."

"Baloney. You and Mom pray for me. God's going to answer your prayers. . ."

"Aurora. You know better than that!"

"You really want to tell me about men. . .birds and bees . . . sex, that stuff, don't you?" She got up and posed in the lamplight, draping herself provocatively over the arm of a chair. "I am beautiful. I like men. I like to have them touch me, kiss me, hold me. It makes me feel alive. . ."

"You are too young. . ."

"Daddy, don't be so naive. I'm not going to give you a grandchild. I'm not stupid!"

"You cheapen yourself. You ruin your chances of getting a good man. . ."

She started dancing around to some unheard music. "But it's such fun . . ."

"You've been drinking."

"Only a teensy bit of champagne. Only the best for your gorgeous daughter."

"Aurora, I love you . . ."

"Yeah, Dad, I know that whole sermon too."

"But a college football player is too old . . ."

"What a bore! I had to fight him off. Just trying to make Teddy jealous, and it worked. Teddy brought me home."

She came and dropped on her knees in front of him, suddenly sober. "Daddy, I do love you. I tease you a lot, but don't believe all I say. I can't help it. Momma wants me to be so perfect. She wants to run every minute of my life. She won't let me alone. I get fed up. I get so I can't take it even if I do understand. I won't do anything to disgrace you. I will be careful. I'm sorry I disobeyed you tonight and said those awful things. I did go to a concert tonight with Teddy, but I need you to chew me out once in a while. Do you love me as much as you love Gracie?"

"You know I do."

She was in his arms. "I was so worried when you were sick. Please get well." She kissed him. "May I help you upstairs?"

"You go on, Honey. I can make it."

She threw him a kiss as she left.

He had noticed her smeared make-up, her tangled hair, her extremely low neckline, her bare legs and feet, her short skirt. He had a strong feeling she had manipulated him again. She acted just like Julia. She listened, responded as he wished, and then completely ignored what he was trying to say.

Yet, for one moment he had also seen her need for him and his love and her deep need for God. He fell asleep, praying.

CHAPTER XI
Escape

Julia sat at the kitchen table alone. Her hands were circling a white mug of cold coffee. The rest of the family had already gone to bed. She wanted to sit, savoring the thoughts of the perfect evening a little longer. Aurora's graduation had been splendid. Who had taken scholastic honors? Aurora! Who had looked like a perfect angel as she sang an elaborate aria with the full orchestra? Aurora!

The white graduation robe had worried her at first. Aurora needed more color to look her best, but it had been no problem. The money spent on modeling and charm courses were certainly worth it. Aurora was skilled at using make-up and beauty aids. She had looked like a frost princess, sparkling, scintillating, gorgeous.

Julia basked in remembering the standing ovation after her solo. Edward had not felt well. He had seemed pale and uncomfortable all evening.

Albert Viert had accepted Julia's invitation to come

and shared her pride in his prize pupil. He had spoken with Julia and Edward for a few moments after the program about a special audition he was arranging for Aurora with some friends of his. There was a very good possibility for a full paid year of study in Europe, an open door to opera, classical music, and sure fame. He asked them to call him the next Monday.

Here was the break Julia had been dreaming of all her life. She couldn't wait to tell Aurora.

Julia had wanted to give a reception for Aurora after the graduation, but Aurora had flatly refused. A group of seniors were going to a resort on the ocean for the next two days. She would be gone until Friday. There would be no time for a reception then because Saturday night was Jon's wedding. Julia slammed the mug on the table spilling some of the cold coffee on the plastic table top. She deeply resented the fact that the bride and her family had arranged everything ignoring her except to ask what she was to wear. She did like the rose crepe dress Grace had made for her.

What really irked her was that the Tylers had not asked Aurora to participate in the wedding at all, not even to sing. Grace would play the prelude and be a bridesmaid. But Aurora? No.

Julia told herself that it was because Aurora's beauty would outshine everyone, and no bride would like that. But they could at least have asked her to sing! She could have sung from the balcony.

Nancy had tried to explain that the ceremony would not be that formal. They had a friend from college who was especially good with a guitar and had a warm soft voice. He had written special music for the occasion.

Julia made circles in the spilled coffee with her finger. She must forget all of this. Nancy was a dear girl, and Jon was so happy. It was obvious that they were deeply in love. Jon had changed so much during the past year at college. Both of them planned to finish school, and they had direction and goals. Julia was happy for them.

Julia intended to do another thing tonight—write to her mother. She had saved a graduation program and was going to write on it.

Edward was always pressuring her to contact her mother. He had kept in close touch with her but Julia seldom bothered. Ever since Aurora's accident and Grace's sudden early birth, Julia had felt nothing but coldness toward her mother. It was wrong, she knew. Maybe this summer she would go visit her now that she was having so many health problems. Since they would be close maybe she and Aurora could make some contacts in Hollywood while they were there.

She stood to take her cup to the sink and go to bed.

The sound of a key in the lock of the back door startled her. It swung open and Aurora came in followed by Teddy, a tall young man who had often been here.

Aurora was very pale with dark circles under her eyes. Her make-up was smudged. Her white dress was bedraggled, and her hair was mussed. She sank into a chair and put her head in her arms on the table.

Teddy spoke anxiously. "She's sick, Mrs. Justin. We were going away, but I thought she had better come home."

"Yeah, Mom. We were going to Nevada to be married, but I heaved and heaved. I came home to get some other clothes. How come you're up?"

"To elope. . .?"

"Yes, Mom. I'm pregnant."

"Aurora, you're. . ."

"Mrs. Justin, we thought it would be best to go away to be married. You see, I love Aurora. . ."

"Get out! Leave at once!" Julia flew at him, arms flailing, screaming in anger.

Aurora was laughing. "Go on, Teddy. I'll handle her. We can go tomorrow when I feel better. Call me." She pushed him out the door, throwing him a kiss.

It took several minutes for Aurora to get Julia calmed down and seated at the table. By then Edward and Grace joined them looking bewildered and alarmed.

Julia couldn't quit sobbing, and Edward took her in his arms.

"Please explain," he asked Aurora.

"I came home to get some other clothes. Mom was up and tried to stop us."

"Us?"

"Teddy and me."

"You were going to the senior party?"

"No. We were going to elope."

"You and Teddy?"

"Yes. I'm pregnant," she said matter-of-factly.

Aurora laughed at their startled responses. She got them to sit at the table again. Grace perched on the kitchen stool by the sink.

Julia blew her nose and looked up. "You are not getting married. No way! That is what I did, and I won't let you wreck your life."

"Mom, that's ridiculous," Aurora said patting her hand. "Your life wasn't ruined."

"Oh, yes, it was. I could have been a concert pianist. A great one. I could have. . ."

"Now, Julia. . ." Edward said. He'd heard this story before.

"I won't let you do it."

"Mom, I love Teddy. I'm going to have his baby."

"How do you know it's his?" Grace asked sarcastically.

Aurora swung to face her. "You stay out of this and keep your mouth shut."

Edward held up his hand. "Stop. All of you. This is very serious. We must face it calmly."

"Calmly? Calmly!" Julia screamed. "There is only one thing to do. We will do it. Now. Tonight. Aurora go change your clothes. I will go pack. We are leaving. Now."

"Julia, stop."

"We will go to Los Angeles. You have an appointment there, a film test, an audition, something for an excuse. We will stay there. We will go to my Mother's. I must pack." She left through the swinging door.

The other three were silent.

Edward took off his glasses and rubbed his wrinkled forehead. "Aurora, we must think this through."

"Daddy, I'm sorry." She went to hug him. "I do love Teddy. I want to have his baby."

"And give up a brilliant career," Grace added. "And clean house, and wash diapers, and scrub and iron, and do dishes three times a day, and stay home, annd have no money . . ."

"You shut up!"

"You have a responsibility to your unborn child . . ." Edward began.

"Oh, Daddy, I know," Aurora said sweetly. "You will talk to Mother, won't you?"

"Yes, of course." He stood up and went to find Julia.

Muttering and groaning she was throwing her things into a large suitcase. Her face was red, swollen, and tear-streaked.

"Julia, Dear, you can't go now. We'll find a solution."

"Edward, just stay out of my way!"

"But, Jon's wedding. You must be there."

"Jon's wedding? Oh, yes. I forgot. No . . . I . . . we . . . have to go now, before anyone finds out."

"Teddy is a good man. He has something to say about this. We have to be fair to him."

"Teddy? That fiend! Taking advantage of a young innocent girl! He should be horse whipped . . . or sued . . . or . . ."

"Julia!"

"Get out of my way! I'm leaving, and I'm taking Aurora with me. How you handle the rest of it is up to you. There is no way to stop me. No way." She jammed the suitcase shut. "I want the bank book and what cash you have. Now."

The suitcase was too heavy for her to carry. She pushed it to the head of the stairs and let it roll down. She ignored the fresh gashes in the paint and wall paper.

Running to Aurora's room, she grabbed an armload of clothing, and pushed past Edward in the hallway as he tried to reason with her. As she hurried down the stairs, she almost fell.

There was nothing to do but help her. Aurora just shrugged and gave in to her mother. In half an hour the car was packed, and Julia and Aurora left without waving or looking back.

The next day Edward spent several hours with Teddy in the church office. Aurora never saw him again.

Jon and Nancy were married in a lovely worshipful service. Edward performed the ceremony. The music reflected their joyous spirit and love. Some polite inquiries were made about the missing family members, but the occasion was so happy for everyone that they were scarcely missed.

CHAPTER XII

Choice

Edward sat in his easy chair, feet propped up, reading the evening paper. There it was in print, Grace was taking high honors in her graduating class and was to receive a valuable scholarship.

Tonight she was out again with Gary Kimball, this time to a sports event in San Francisco. To have her with a man he trusted completely no matter how late they stayed out was a good feeling for Edward. Grace was quite popular and dated several young men. Although Gary was older than the others, Edward hoped he would be the one to win Grace's love.

The headline article on the front page of the paper carried Gary's by-line. He had worked his way up on the staff of the local paper and had the potential for a successful career.

The house was very quiet. He hadn't even turned on the T.V. He stretched and yawned.

Three years had passed since Julia had left so hastily with Aurora. How time had whizzed by.

Thanks to Grace, they had been good years. She had managed the household tasks efficiently. A peaceful routine that was good for both of them had been established. He felt better than he had for years.

Now he had much more time for his church work, and it was going well. They had just hired a young couple to be youth ministers. It seemed probable that the church would be building an addition soon.

As Grace grew older, her ministry at church grew. She did all the musical accompaniment in an efficient, self-effacing manner, and she also helped sponsor the junior high group. Yet he couldn't help think of how much he missed Julia every day. At first she had been home every other week, or he had gone down to Pasadena during the week to where Julia and Aurora were staying with Julie's mother.

There had never been any sign of Aurora's pregnancy. He had asked Julia, and asked. Finally she was forced to use the ugly word abortion, cutting a wound in Edward that would never heal.

About a year after they left, Julia had called to report that Aurora had a contract with a recording company and that several other prospects were looking good. Money was beginning to flow in. They would move to an apartment in Beverly Hills. Julia's excitement was uncontrolled. "Edward, she has made it! You have no idea. . ."

"I miss you, Julia."

"I know. I miss you, too."

That scene was replayed over and over in the next year. By the third year he had learned to accept and not expect.

The church family seemed to understand Julia's absence and support him. At first there had been some gossip, so he had called a special meeting of the church board and in a closed session had told them of his problems. Instead of condemning him and asking him to leave they formed a circle around him and, literally, covered him with their prayers. He would be eternally grateful to those wonderful people. Instead of gossip, everyone's attention became fixed on the love which the church members had for one another. Many new people were drawn to the congregation by it. The talk had ceased and many people were even following Aurora's career with interest.

It had been at least a year since Aurora had been home. According to Julia, her agent had more bookings for her than she could handle.

Financially things were better, also. Lately, he had not had to spend any savings. Aurora's earnings took care of everything in the expensive Beverly Hills apartment.

Edward took up the paper again. He planned to go to the hospital to see Mrs. Greeley. She was recovering nicely. Today her family would probably be with her, so he would go tomorrow. He stretched, thinking of fixing himself some tea.

He heard a car turn into the driveway and stop. The car doors slammed in a way he had almost forgotten. He had expected Jon and Nancy to come by with baby Eddie.

"Hey, Pops, where are you?" Aurora was calling!

He hurried to meet them in the kitchen. Julia rushed into his arms. He held her, reluctant to let go.

A tall, long-haired, handsome, older man was with them. He was loaded down with luggage.

"Pops, meet Henry Cable. He drove us up from L.A. He has business in San Francisco. Put that stuff over there, Henry. Pick me up after noon tomorrow. We will have the long drive back just to ourselves." She threw her arms around him and kissed him passionately. She eased him out the back door.

When Aurora returned she kissed Edward on the forehead, and went to sit on the kitchen stool. It seemed like a dream to Edward. She was a beautiful, unreal picture, every line and color too perfect. She had hardened, and her eyes were guarded and aware. Her black, fitted dress accented every move.

"It's so good to see you," he said, finally shaking himself into reality. You both look lovely. Julia, I love the way you stay so slim and attractive!" He pulled her onto his lap.

She beamed at him. "It is good to be home. I miss you, Edward."

"Knock it off, you two," Aurora said smiling, happy to see them together. "Where is my brainy sister?"

"She's out with Gary Kimball. Remember him?"

"Sure do. Faithful old puppy dog, how is he? Isn't he a little old for Gracie?"

"They seem to get along well. He is not her only escort."

"Well, good for her! I expected that she would do well without my competition. I'm tired. Guess I'll go up and shower. How about bringing up my bags, Pop?"

Julia glanced at her watch. "Your commercial should be on the next T.V. show. I want you to see it, Edward. She got paid plenty for making it."

"Aw, Mom, you've seen it ten dozen times. It's lousy. Forget it."

"Have you seen it, Edward?"

"No."

"You must." Julia hurried into the living room.

"Good to see you, Pops. How are you?" Aurora put her arms around him. She smelled of some strange exotic musk.

"I'm fine, Honey. How are you?"

"Great! Just super great! Rich and in demand." She whirled away and picked up her cosmetics case.

He followed her upstairs with two heavy suitcases and then returned to sit by Julia on the couch in the livingroom.

He put his arm around her and she cuddled against him, but her concentration was on the glowing screen.

"The commercial should be on now. Yes, it's beginning. Watch now. There she is."

Aurora came floating onto the screen in a cloud of pink chiffon. She posed by a sleek silver car and spoke her lines in a lilting voice. Then her voice soared into an intricate singing pattern that was quite provocative. A close-up showed rich full lips and a suggestive wink.

Edward felt cold inside. The girl on the screen could not be his daughter. But she was.

"Isn't she great, Edward?"

"Rather sexy . . ."

"I know. Hasn't her voice improved?"

He went to switch off the T.V. and returned to sit close beside Julia, his arms around her.

"When are you coming back, Love?"

"I am back, Dear."

"I mean to stay."

"Just a little longer now. You see, Edward, Aurora needs my restraining influence. She gets too involved. Late parties, early calls. She forgets to rest. Also, she must practice and get to her lessons on time."

"She does have an agent, and a social secretary."

"But she still needs me."

"More than I do?"

"Edward, we have discussed this so many times. You know how I feel. God gave us our daughter. We have kept the faith. She is so successful."

He groaned aloud but let it pass. "I'm glad you came for Grace's graduation. It will mean a lot to her."

"Aurora can't stay. She has to be back for an audition."

"That figures!"

"Are you bitter, Edward?"

"Not really, Dear. I am anxious about the way you are living. You do get to church, I hope."

"Not often. Sunday is our only day to relax."

"Are you forgetting that God must come first?"

"Now, Edward, you don't need to preach to me."

"I hope not. Just don't forget to have the proper perspective . . ."

"You are preaching!"

"Honey, I'm concerned for you and for Aurora."

"That is ridiculous. I'm taking care of her. We're doing fine. I haven't even asked for money for ages."

"That is not what I mean. When did you pray with Aurora last?"

"Pray? With Aurora?" She was quiet a moment. Then she turned and kissed him, as if to do so would smooth over everything. "Don't you worry, Dear. I'm home now. Everything is great."

He sighed. "But you cannot stay. . ."

"Soon, Dear, soon. There is a good chance for a long term contract. Maybe then. Let's go have some coffee. I have so much to tell you."

They settled at the kitchen table. Edward scarcely listened as Julia told in detail of the glamorous life she was leading. He barely recognized famous names and places.

There was an unpleasant, hot tightness in his stomach. Nothing seemed to have changed, even after his many prayers!

Much later Grace and Gary Kimball came through the back door. They were surprised and pleased to see Julia.

"Mother, you came for my graduation!"

"Of course, Dear. Didn't you expect me?"

"You are so busy."

"I'm proud of you, Grace, taking honors and all. How are you, Gary?"

"Fine, Mrs. Justin. Busy at the paper."

"Have you seen Jon lately?"

"I see them often. That grandson of yours is some boy!"

"I do miss seeing him."

"Did Aurora come?" Grace asked.

"I sure did." She entered in a thin pale peach negligee trimmed with feathers. "Hi. Why hello, Gary. Haven't seen you for ages." She went to him and kissed him on the lips.

Gently he pushed her away but kept one arm around her. "Quite a greeting!"

"I still love you, Gary."

Grace gave her dad a look and went to sit beside him at the table.

"It is good to see you all," Gary said. "I must go. Call you tomorrow, Grace. Good night all." He made a hasty exit.

Grace didn't move.

Aurora was laughing. "Oh, Sis, I can still get to you. Poor Gary."

"That was in very poor taste," Edward stated. "Especially since you are practically nude."

"Don't you like my outfit, Daddy? Cost plenty." She whirled around. "Most men like it." She came and put her arms around him and kissed his bald spot. "You are the same old square, and I love you. Hey, Grace, come upstairs. I have a super graduation gift for you. Got it at an exclusive boutique on Sunset Boulevard. You'll love it. Come on. Let's talk."

They left the kitchen with Aurora chatting happily.

Edward sat, unmoving.

Julia took his hand. "Edward, I want to take Grace back with me. I think she should have her chance."

"Chance for what?"

"She is attractive and very good on the piano. With my connections I could get her a good job."

"But she has one."

"Working with old people! Playing bingo with them, helping them make pot holders!"

"Julia, don't mock. She likes it, and they love her."

"I'm at least going to ask her to go."

"It is her choice. I have confidence that she will make the right decision."

Edward hurt deep inside when he took Grace and Julia to the airport a few days later. Grace was excited and glowing. She was going to taste a new world of glamour, glitter, and action. As he kissed her goodbye he slipped an envelope in her leather bag. It contained a return ticket and two twenty dollar bills.

Two weeks passed slowly. Edward tried to stay active, but the silent, empty house was always waiting for him at the end of the day.

He spent many hours with Jon, Nancy, and little Eddie. That grandson was the most . . . the most! Like other proud grandfathers, words failed him.

He met Gary Kimball for lunch one day. While they

talked Edward realized how important Grace was to Gary. Edward was not surprised when Gary said he loved Grace and asked permission to propose to her. They laughed together at the old fashioned formality, but Edward was pleased and flattered and gave his consent. He expressed his hope that Grace would go to college. Amazingly, Gary wished the same thing and said he would be willing to wait or work it out, as Grace desired.

Edward went home that night with a warm feeling. Gary Kimball was a good man. He would enjoy having him for a son-in-law. If Grace . . .

The phone rang.

"Hi, Daddy."

"Grace, Love. Just thinking of you. When are you coming home?"

"Don't know, Daddy. I'm playing the piano as a guest artist at the place where Aurora sings."

"Where's that, Honey?"

"It's a place called the Sea View Ballroom."

"A night club?"

"Not exactly."

"Do they have a bar?"

"Well, yes."

"Honey, . . . "

"Don't say it, Daddy. You can trust me."

"But . . . "

"I'm having a ball, Daddy. Aurora has bought me a bunch of new clothes. Mom is a dear. I like it here. There's a neat guy. I'll come see you soon. Honest."

He hung up slowly. Icy cold fear swept over him like a cascade. She even sounded differently, more brittle.

The next two days he just couldn't concentrate on anything. He wanted to drive straight to Los Angeles and bring her back. Wisely, he knew that was the wrong thing to do. If she came back, it would have to be her decision.

He drove far into the redwoods and spent a day alone, praying and meditating.

On his way back he stopped to see Mrs. Greeley at her home. Her granddaughter was staying with her while she was recuperating. They insisted that he stay for dinner. He enjoyed the pleasant company and excellent food. They gave him a box of cookies to take with him.

When he left, Mrs. Greeley went to the door with him. "Reverend, how are things at home?"

"It looks like I have lost Grace."

"Where is your faith and trust?"

"Wearing very thin."

"Could it be that you are trying to shoulder too much?"

"Could you . . . do you have time to talk a few minutes?" he asked.

They sat together on the front steps.

"Things too much for you, Reverend?"

"Three years, Mrs. Greeley. And now Grace is gone, too. How can I understand God's timing?"

"No one can."

"I know that, but it hurts so much. What did I do wrong? I tried to help each one of my family commit themselves to Jesus Christ. I thought each of them had. But . . ."

"Reverend, you can't do it for anyone. Each has to make a personal choice and commitment."

"Julia says we have done a good job with Aurora. We have 'developed her God-given potential,' but you've seen her, Mrs. Greeley. She's hard and brittle and selfish. She has all the wrong attributes. I'm afraid Julia does, too."

"Julia has gone her own way, Reverend. She will have to answer for herself."

"I know, but I still feel so guilty. I keep seeing that verse in First Timothy, chapter 5, verse eight, that says if we don't take care of our own family we have denied the faith and are worse than unbelievers."

"Do you feel you have denied the faith? Look at your successful church work."

"No. I have kept the faith. But how much greater would my influence and outreach be if my family were a witness too?"

"God knows."

"I feel inadequate and weak."

"Yet, you still pray. Can't you trust? There is also a verse in Matthew that invites you to let Jesus Christ help you carry your heavy load and give you rest."

"You are right." He stood up, feeling renewed by her gentle encouragement. "I must not keep you. Thank you, Mrs. Greeley, for the dinner and for so much more. I will never be able to repay you."

"My payment comes from a higher source, Reverend. Your friendship means much to me. I will continue to pray for you and your family."

He nodded and went to the car and drove away.

It was after dark when he reached their street. As the house came into view, he could see a light in the kitchen.

Grace met him at the back door with a hug and a bright smile. "Surprise! Daddy, I'm home."

He greeted her joyfully. "Did Mom come? Aurora?"

"No. Just me."

They sat at the kitchen table. He poured milk for them and they munched Mrs. Greeley's cookies.

"Tell me all about it, Grace."

"I'd rather not, Daddy." There was a shadow in her eyes. She had grown up since he had seen her last.

"Bad experience?"

"I liked it. I liked the weather, the new clothes, plenty of money, exciting happenings and people. I liked the attention I got when I could play any requests they asked. I liked going places with famous people until . . . until . . . " She took a deep breath. "I got scared. I left suddenly. Mom will be mad at me. I just can't explain."

"I think I understand. Thank God!"

"I would have lost . . . lost all I believe in. All you have taught me. I couldn't stay."

"You won't ever be sorry." He held her hands across the table. "Welcome home."

"It is so good to be here. Thank you for putting that ticket and money in my bag."

"I am so thankful! By the way, there is someone else who will be glad you are home."

She smiled. "Gary? I've missed him too. I'll call him tomorrow."

CHAPTER XIII

Decision

After the morning service Edward went straight to his office in the new wing of the church. He shut the door and sat at his desk with his head in his hands. Completely uninspired, his message had been a well-organized nothing!

The gray fog that enveloped him constantly would not lift, not even when he tried to pray. Life was only a routine he followed by habit.

Without conscious volition he rolled a piece of paper into the typewriter. Before his eyes a resignation produced itself. With shaking fingers he signed it, folded it, put it in an envelope and held it. Minutes passed as he held it. Finally he slid it into his inside coat pocket and left the church without speaking to anyone.

When he got home he packed a suitcase. He left a note for Grace on the kitchen table in case she might come home from Cal. State.

He locked the house. Mr. Kimball was in his yard. Edward called to him and asked him to keep an eye on the place. He drove away, taking the highway that would connect with Interstate 5 going south.

It was late when he arrived, and the parking area at the apartment building in Beverly Hills was full. Edward parked two blocks away in a closed gas station and walked back. He was extremely tired and had eaten very little. He felt weak and dizzy.

Someone in the apartment complex was throwing a party. People swarmed all over the patio and pool areas. A strange man pushed a drink into his hand, greeting him noisily and drunkenly.

Julia and Aurora lived in Apartment 2, but he couldn't even get there through the crowd.

Edward found a canvas chair in the semi-darkness under the balcony. He poured his drink into a planter beside him.

As he sat looking into the noisy torch-lit scene he saw Julia. A man had his arm around her, and she was laughing up into his face. She looked like a stranger with her hair piled high and a tightly fitting long dark blue dress outlining her slim body.

A series of musical chords from a piano cut the noise a bit.

"Aurora, Baby, let's hear some music."

"Give us a preview, Doll. Something from your new movie."

Edward heard her brittle laugh. The spotlight outlined his daughter as she stood by the piano. The neck line of her black dress plunged below her waist. A single scintillating gem reflected light from deep between her breasts. Her long silver hair hung freely as she swayed with the first words of an off-beat rhythm.

Edward felt sick. His stomach hurt, and cold sweat broke out on his forehead. He wanted to leave but he was unable to move.

Her low, seductive voice picked up the tempo. The guests were moving in rhythm, making wild shadow patterns in the torchlight. Someone laughed nervously. A glass fell and broke on the pavement.

Aurora ended on a high note that faded into a whisper. Everyone clapped wildly, shouting for more.

"Sorry, dear fans, the next songs will cost you money at the Blue Grotto in Santa Monica. Let's go!"

Within minutes the crowd diminished. As Julia went out the gate with her escort, Edward called to her.

She turned in alarm. "Edward, what a surprise! You should have called. We have to leave." She was nervous and confused.

"I just thought I would come and see you."

"Here. Take my key. We will be home late. Aurora's last appearance is at 3 A.M. Make yourself at home." She didn't even introduce him.

The lights came on, and the caterers began to clear away the remains of the party. "You care for something, Sir?" one of them asked him politely.

"No, thank you." He knew he should eat, but the remains on the table repulsed him. The odor of alcohol was overpowering.

He found the apartment, and let himself in. The door wasn't even locked. He switched on lights and wandered around. The deep shag carpets, and plush furniture in shades of blue and gold were accented by many mirrors and lamps. The kitchen was bare and the refrigerator empty, except for an unfinished T.V. dinner and a bottle of ginger ale. He poured a glass half full and found some snack crackers.

There were two bedrooms. The larger one was a scattered mess with clothing, cosmetics, music, and pictures cluttering the walls, open wardrobes, tables and floor. It was typical of Aurora.

Hesitantly, he looked in the other bedroom. It was neat and straight. Nothing in it reminded him of Julia.

He sat on the low couch. The crackers tasted like sand, and the ginger ale was flat. There was no place for him here. He ached with weariness and needed food.

He dropped the key on the table by the door, turned out the lights, and left. He had passed a motel and cafe a few miles back. Perhaps things would look differently tomorrow.

At ten A.M. he called, and Julia's very sleepy voice informed him that he shouldn't come back until at least two o'clock. No one would be up until then.

He drove to Santa Monica and had lunch near the pier. He got directions to the Blue Grotto. The location was on the beach south of the city. In daylight it looked lifeless and sordid. The garish paintings looked dull and overdrawn. If this was where Aurora made her appearances, she had a long way to go to make it to the top, or not far to go to reach bottom.

He walked along the palisade park trying to relax and shake off the depression he felt setting in. At least the scenery was superb and the sunshine was warm and pleasant.

He stopped to sit on a bench. A small boy was playing on the swings near by. His father was pushing him higher and higher. They were laughing. Edward was reminded of Jonathan and his young son, Eddie. He saw them often and was always thankful for the miracles that had saved Jon from disaster. Grace, Gary, and Mrs. Greeley deserved much credit. They had provided the love that kept bringing him home during his rebellious years.

He thought of Grace. He should call her, but she would not approve of this trip. She was worried about his health. And she had reason enough, although he had not told her. The doctor's last report had not been good. Restrictions had been placed on him again, but he found it almost impossible to follow them.

He hoped that Grace would marry Gary Kimball. She kept putting him off. Something held her back.

The boy and the father he had been watching ran off together. Edward looked at his watch, time to head back to Beverly Hills.

He prayed as he drove. He needed Julia. Her infrequent visits home were not enough. Now he needed her, so much. He needed the right words to convince her. He was even prepared to live with her here. He would give up everything, even find another job. The loneliness was more than he could bear. He thought of the letter of resignation in his suit pocket at the motel.

This time he parked close to the beautifully landscaped apartment complex. The white stucco and red tile was impressive. Several people lounged by the pool.

Aurora, lovely in a bright orange sun dress, came running to him, followed by the same dark, long-haired man who had brought her home that time. Was his name Cable? Yes, Henry Cable.

"Hi, Daddy." She hugged him. "Have to leave for rehearsal. See you." She gave him a quick kiss and ran on past.

"Rev. Justin," the man said, saluting him.

Julia was standing in the apartment door in attractive blue silk hostess pajamas.

"Hello, Edward. Sorry we were in such a hurry last night. I didn't ask you along because I knew you wouldn't want to come since they serve liquor. Do come in." She gave him a kiss on the cheek and slid out of his arms. She led the way in. "Can I get you something?

Coffee, tea, something stronger?" She laughed and sat on the couch with one leg tucked under her.

"Julia, I've come to take you home," he blurted, "or move in here with you."

"Sit down, Edward, here, by me."

The gold phone at her elbow rang. She smiled at him and picked it up.

"Oh, Tony. Yes, my husband is here. . . Oh, no. That shouldn't make any difference. I'm sure he won't mind. . . I do want to see if Aurora does as well tonight as she did last night . . . She was, wasn't she? . . . Yes, I'm proud . . . Sky's the limit . . . Right. Usual time? I'll be waiting."

"Julia . . ."

"You won't mind if I go out, Edward? I had an invitation for dinner. You should have called. I could have planned differently."

"Julia, I've come to take you home, or to arrange something else."

"Now, Edward . . ."

"You have put me off for three years, Julia. I need you. I want you. I love you. You are still my wife."

The phone rang again.

"Hello . . . Thank you . . . She was wonderful, wasn't she? . . . Yes, I'll tell her."

"Honey . . ."

"The phone has just been ringing all day, Edward. The new movie is just beginning to gain attention. I must tell you about it. Isn't it exciting? You should hear her sing. She has improved so much. What control! Come with us tonight."

"The Blue Grotto? No, Dear. I can't go to places like that."

"Not even to hear your daughter sing?"

"My daughter? Have you noticed how she has changed? Have you really looked at her? And yourself?"

"How cruel, Edward! How can you say such things?"

"It looks to me like you and Aurora have sold out . . . to the devil."

"Edward!" She stood and faced him angrily.

"Julia." He held out his hand. "Please come with me. I love you."

"You are out of your mind. How can you say those things?"

"Please come back to me. Grace will be leaving me soon. I am not well. Julia?"

She looked at him, then she looked around the room. She caught her reflection in several mirrors and began to laugh. He took off his glasses and wiped his forehead, then wiped his eyes and replaced his glasses. When he closed the door behind him, she was still laughing.

He checked out of the motel and drove through the city. He saw the signs marking the turn off to the Pasadena Freeway and followed the traffic.

Without thinking, he found his way to his mother-in-law's house. It had been a long time since he had visited her. They had kept in touch by phone and letter over the years. He admired her in every way. She greeted him lovingly and showed her pleasure and surprise. She had aged and was bent, but she was neat and attractive with white hair, sparkling blue eyes, and a sunny smile.

He relaxed immediately as she fussed over him and made him comfortable.

He noticed that she was packing. "You have made a decision to move?"

"Yes, Edward. This place has become too much for

me alone. I have found a retirement community that I like. Many of my friends are there, and it is a great place. I know I can be happy there."

"Can you handle it financially?"

"Yes, Edward. Thank you for asking. I have already mailed the letter to you explaining what I plan to do. I hope you approve."

"Of course. Now I know why I was directed here. I am going to help you move!" He took off his jacket. "Where do we begin?"

"Oh, thank you. I have friends helping me at odd times. They are great, but I have a whole lifetime of things to sort through. Everything is so heavy for me."

They worked side by side and found themselves laughing and joking.

After a leisurely dinner they sat longer at the lunch counter in the kitchen.

"Why didn't you ask Julia to come help you move?" Edward asked.

"Oh, I couldn't do that."

"Why not?"

"She is much too busy. Thank you for making her come see me and straighten out our differences. At least we are friends now."

"I'm glad."

"Now, Edward, why are you here?"

He got up and went into the front room. He stood looking out the curtainless window.

She came and stood beside him. "Can you tell me about it, Son?"

They sat beside each other on the couch. Tears filled his eyes. "I came to see if Julia would go home with me. I am ready to give up my job and move down here. I can't think. I can't even pray anymore."

"It is Julia. You still love her? I can see how she has changed."

"I need her. I can't stand to be alone."

"No, Son, you don't need Julia. You need God. He never leaves us alone."

"What?"

Her blue eyes held compassion and love.

"I need. . .God?"

"You have shouldered your family's burdens too long."

"My burden is not light. Mrs. Greeley told me that."

"Exactly. Each of us has to answer for our own choices: you, Julia, Jon, Aurora, Grace, and me. It is an individual thing."

"But I am responsible for my family. It was my duty to teach each of them the right way. I failed, and that makes me guilty."

"You have not failed, Edward. You have always been a caring and loving father to your family. You may have made mistakes. God forgives, you know that."

"I need God? I am a minister. I have always had Him."

She put her hand on his arm. "Then why is your burden of guilt so heavy and your loneliness so unbearable?"

He sat wrapped in silence. She left him there alone.

He stayed several days, helping her settle in her new home. They talked and prayed together often and long. He found it easy to tell her his anxieties, and she listened sympathetically.

He ate regularly and slept long hours. When he headed home there was relief from his foggy state. He immersed himself in work and found that he could help people again.

But he still could not help himself. His guilt became heavier as Aurora's fame grew.

She had starred in a musical that became an immediate success. Her picture was on the front covers of national magazines. She was interviewed on all the talk shows. She was a guest on one T.V. variety show after another, singing and dancing. The reviews declared that she was one of the most versatile performers the entertainment world had ever seen.

Since she had kept her own name, Aurora Justin, there was no escape for Edward. He was notorious because he was her father. He was constantly being approached to give interviews, be photographed, and sign autographs. Grace insisted that he was being stuffy and square about the whole thing. God could use people in any profession. The entertainment field was an excellent one to enter and serve God.

Edward agreed, but he sensed something wrong. When people talked with him about Aurora, there was a hesitancy that he couldn't explain.

Grace tried to get him to go see the movie. When he kept putting it off she went with Gary. When they returned, Grace was quiet until Gary said goodnight.

She kneeled by Edward's chair. "Daddy, don't go to Aurora's movie."

"Why not, Honey?"

"The music is beautiful. In fact the whole thing is spectacular in every way, but it is rated R. Even I was embarrassed, Daddy."

He did not go.

Julia phoned Edward almost daily, ecstatic. Then she made a breathless, hurried visit home to announce that Aurora was marrying Henry Cable. He had directed her movie success. He was the top of the most eligible bachelor list! He was a multi-millionare! Julia raved on and on.

She was planning the wedding of the century. It was her right as mother of the bride. Everything was to be traditional and money was no object. Henry Cable was paying for everything.

She stayed just long enough to alert each member of her family as to what she expected of them during this time. Just before she left, Julia abruptly told Edward she was never going to come home again to this stuffy small town. Life here was too dull and unexciting. After the wedding he could forget her. She had other things to do.

Edward watched her as she drove off in her bright orange sports car. He would not wave good-bye. Then he went to his office and wrote a letter to church headquarters requesting a transfer and explaining his position. He hoped the church could use him in some capacity.

CHAPTER XIV
Wedding

Crowds of people ignored the coolness of the December evening as, an hour before the wedding, they lined the velvet cord barriers in front of the immense brick church on Wilshire Boulevard. Police held up lines of traffic as two long limousines turned into the driveway and halted at the temporary gates. Guards in uniforms of Global Film Studios let the cars through and saluted as they passed.

The T.V. crew arrived and set up their equipment on special scaffolding. They tried to take long-range pictures, but they were unsuccessful. Aurora Justin, the bride, was completely concealed in a black fur hooded cape as she made her quick entrance into the side door of the church surrounded by relatives and friends.

"Hey, this is like a royal wedding or a movie premier," one of the reporters remarked. "Haven't seen anything like this since the good old days. What a production! All we need is a brass band or two." As if to respond, the church chimes began to play. The crew laughed, but then turned to their work.

A silver Rolls convertible drove up, depositing Henry Cable, the groom. The newsmen found it easy to locate information about him. He practically owned Global Films, Inc. He was famous for directing and producing fabulous extravaganzas in his unique style. Aurora Justin had reached stardom in the latest one. Her acting talent was equalled by her fabulous voice and beauty.

Aurora had charmed Henry Cable. They had been a twosome for some time. The gossips had speculated as to them to whether they would ever make it legal. He had been an eligible bachelor for several years following his second divorce. Questions floated through the crowd. Would his former wives be here? How about the two grown and married sons and the daughter who was the same age as the bride?

In a small, windowless Sunday School room in the basement of the church Edward Justin, father of the bride, waited alone. He pulled at his cravat. Maybe someone would have a minute to help him fold it correctly. His rented deep green velvet tuxedo was a bit tight across the shoulders. He adjusted the gold embroidered vest. His cumerbund was in a wad around his middle.

He was sitting on a small red table. Primary chairs in bright colors were set against the wall. Posters and mottoes took the place of windows. In the center of the front wall was a large framed and colored picture of Christ with His open hands reaching out in love. The caption read: "Come unto me."

He had been weeping inside for days, especially since he had come to Southern California and stayed in the motel. Jon, Nancy, Eddie, and Grace had been with him and were wonderful; but there was no one to understand his deepest feelings.

Pictures of his daughter at different stages in her life kept floating through his mind. First, as he had held Aurora in her newborn perfection. She had looked up at him in utter trust as he had dedicated her to God, giving her back to Him in thankfulness. How he had failed as a father!

He could never in his wildest dreams have imagined the beautiful, cold, self-centered, sex symbol she had become. How did he let it happen? When should he have stopped all this?

What a weak spineless person he had been! He had always let Julia have her own way just to avoid conflict and argument. How stupid and gutless!

Through his failure he had lost both Julia and his daughter. All he could see ahead for them both was disaster, unhappiness, and ruin. As much as he loved them, he felt no power to avert the tragedy. He tried to pray but God seemed far from the scene of the cinema-filled production that was taking place around him.

"Oh, there you are, Dad." Grace pushed open the door. "We've been looking for you. Mom wants you there. It's almost time."

She came to him and quickly arranged his cravat and cumberbund.

"Thanks, Honey."

She kissed him on both cheeks. "It's going to be okay, Daddy. We will get through it. Tomorrow we can go home."

"Right. Tomorrow." He straightened his shoulders. "You look lovely, Grace."

"Thanks, Dad. I feel half-naked, and the rest squeezed in." She posed, the dark green velvet enhancing her flawless skin. "It won't look so bad when we get our flowers. It won't matter what we look like anyway. No one will look at anyone but the bride. Come on, Dad; let's get it over with."

She led him down the hall. The lower auditorium was filled with feminine activity. Mirrors, lights, lovely shapes in dark green velvet, hairdressers, make-up artists, assistants—all seemed to be in complete confusion.

In the far corner Aurora stood in front of a full length three-way mirror with several attendents fluttering about. Giggles, laughter, anxiety, nervousness, all mingled in a buzz of sound. A strange perfume pervaded the air.

Julia came hurrying to him, talking constantly, giving orders, checking, completely in her element. She had lived her whole life for this one glorious event. It was as she wished in every detail: traditional, yet sophisticated. Her dreams were realized. She had made them all come true.

"Just a few more minutes, Edward. Remember to walk very slowly . . ." Her words drifted off as she hurried by him to check on something else.

Again memories stirred in Edward. How different she looked from the bride he had led to the altar so many years ago! Her deep wine velvet dress was cut so low and fitted so tightly. She was still young looking, slim, and desirable, but so changed. Only in name did she belong to him, and he must talk to her about that before he went home. Then he saw around her neck the single strand of pearls he had gone into debt to get for her on their special day so long ago.

A woman was taking charge. "Come girls, get in line. Time to get your flowers and go upstairs." There was a flurry of activity. White orchids. Each of the twelve attendants set a single flower in her dark hair and put a lei of white orchids around her neck.

The same provocative scent reached Edward as they went nervously past him to wait on the stairs. He recognized it as the strange musk Aurora always wore.

An usher came to get Julia. She glanced at Edward as she hurried by. Her look was cold and impersonal.

They opened the doors at the top of the stairs and music surrounded them. The deep tones of the organ made the air vibrate, but the music softened to complement Aurora's voice as she sang a love song written especially for the occasion. The guests would think she was singing in person, but Edward could see her standing in front of the mirror for a final time.

Her silver hair hung long around her shoulders with the front pulled high in a puff anchored with a diamond crown. She wore no veil to hide her dark lashes, brows and full lips. Her dress was imported diaphanous silk in palest green embroidered in swirls with seed pearls and tiny diamonds. It was draped Grecian style across the low cut, tightly fitting bodice and swung into a flowing skirt. The train, held by diamond clips at the shoulders, trailed yards behind her. Lace gloves extended above her elbows. Her flowers were a cascade of white and pale green orchids that almost touched the floor.

The music changed, and one by one the bridesmaids went through the doors above. Grace went last, and she whispered as she went past him, "Chin up, Daddy. I love you."

Attendants helped Aurora as she came to join him. Together they carefully ascended the stairs.

"Well, Dad, you'll soon be rid of me," she said as she took his arm.

"I will always be here if you need me, Princess." He breathed a prayer that he would be able to keep that promise.

As they reached the narthex, flash bulbs went off in their faces. Angrily, Aurora waved them away at first, but then she posed for them, realizing they would not be allowed in the sancturary.

For a moment they stood at the threshold. Edward turned to kiss his daughter feeling a deep flow of love. She rebuffed him, murmuring something about her make-up.

The traditional bridal music brought the audience to its feet, and a sea of faces, rapt in admiration, blurred in front of them.

The aisle was miles long and was lit by hundreds of candles.

The familiar ceremony unwound. Soon he sank thankfully beside Julia in the front pew. He felt burning hot inside and frozen outside. His vision blurred. In desperation he prayed.

Aurora was singing the Lord's Prayer in beautiful, unfeeling perfection. Edward thought it was almost sacreligious, but the familiar words began to penetrate his soul.

". . . Thy kingdom come, Thy will be done . . . and forgive us our debts . . . But deliver us from evil . . . For thine is the kingdom, and the power, and the glory . . ."

He lifted his face to the stained glass window behind the altar. It was back-lighted and showed the same picture as the one he had seen in the room below. The face of the Savior glowed, His hands were outstretched in love.

"Cast your burden on the Lord and He will sustain you."

"For my yoke is easy and my burden is light."

Edward felt the guilt inside him melt away as he humbly prayed for forgiveness. He had tried all his life to live as God wanted him to live. And he had failed miserably because he had set the goals himself and tried to follow them in his own strength.

"Forgive mistakes and failures . . . forgive doubt and lack of trust and faith . . . take my burden of guilt . . . become my answer to loneliness . . . take me, a failure as I am . . . I ask in humble faith . . ."

Julia looked at him strangely as she signalled for him to stand. He did not know that his face glowed.

Aurora smiled into the face of her new husband as they passed up the aisle, music soaring. Grace winked at her father as she followed with her escort.

Soon it was Edward's turn to join the procession with Julia. She took his arm, and they followed the wedding party up the long aisle. Edward walked proudly with his beautiful wife, knowing that he still loved her. He leaned toward her and whispered the words to her. She looked at him, startled, and then shrugged slightly. Her interest was in the guests packed into the wooden pews on either side.

There was a roar of noise as they went out the doors of the church. Cameras popped. Reporters, fans, the curious, a jam of people swarmed all over the church yard. Uniformed men cordoned the steps and walk to the long, sleek limousines that pulled away as soon as they were filled, taking the guests to the reception at the exclusive club in the hills above the ocean.

Julia had insisted on a receiving line for guests, although Aurora objected and said it was terribly old-fashioned. Julia won, and they stood for several hours, smiling, welcoming, and receiving congratulations.

Julia seemed to flourish as much as Aurora, her proud groom and the beautiful attendants. Edward finally turned and left. He could stand it no longer. Finding his way through hundreds of dancing, eating, drinking people to the terrace, he stood, leaning on the parapet, and watching the cars on the highway at the foot of the cliff. Just beyond was the restless blackness and roar of the ocean.

"Daddy." Grace held a tray of food and a carafe of steaming coffee. She poured a cup for him and one for herself. "Wow, what a production! Am I tired!" She kicked off her shoes and jumped to sit on the rock wall.

"Thanks, Love."

"Are you okay, Daddy?"

He laughed. "Same worried Grace!"

"Somebody has to take care of you!"

They ate in silence. The hot coffee tasted marvelous.

"Daddy, don't worry about Aurora. She has everything she ever dreamed. Few people attain their goals like she has."

"But they are wrong goals, Grace. I didn't help her at the right time," Edward said, forgetting the forgiveness that had revived him only hours before.

"You did your best, Daddy. If there is anyone to blame, it is Mom. She is the one who led Aurora from the beginning. She was also fulfilling her own dreams."

"Maybe she will be happy, too."

"I doubt it, Daddy. I really doubt it. She will never find happiness away from you and God. You know that, but she will have to find it out for herself."

He nodded, remembering again that God was in control. Then he looked at Grace. "When are you going to marry Gary?"

"Daddy, I . . ."

"Tell me. Has he asked you?"

"Dozens of times."

"You will now?"

"No, Daddy. I just sent him away for good."

"You did what?"

"I told him I could never marry him."

"Why, Honey?"

"You will be alone. The divorce . . . Mom . . . You are sick."

"No longer, Grace. Something happened during the wedding. God spoke to me. I saw how I haven't trusted Him and have tried to do things my own way. How I have failed! How I have punished myself for my failure, but Grace, He forgave me! Even after the mess I have made. He is going to take over and straighten it all out! I am learning what it means to be forgiven."

"Oh, Daddy, that is wonderful!"

"I won't be alone. And it will all work out because God has full control."

"I am so glad!"

"Now, about Gary? I know you love him."

"Yes. Yes, I do, but I sent him away." She was crying. The dim light made diamonds of her tears.

"Grace, I am so sorry. I wish you had told me sooner. You stay right here. Don't you move."

He left her and hurried into the club, shouldering his way through the crowd to the lobby. "Please, God," he prayed. He almost ran to the carpeted exit.

In the floodlight he saw an attendant helping Gary into a taxi. Edward yelled.

Gary turned and came to him. "Sir, are you okay?"

Edward laughed. "You sound like my daughter!" He put his arm across Gary's shoulders and led him back inside.

"Is something wrong, Sir?"

"Yes, indeed. I just found out why you and Grace are not married. Now, you go to her. She is on the terrace. Don't you take no for an answer. I'll perform the ceremony free of charge and with the greatest pleasure. Now go!"

Gary's face lit up. "Thank you, Sir . . . Dad! I'll see to it . . ."

Edward went out and climbed into the taxi alone. He didn't mind at all.

CHAPTER XV
Hope

It was after midnight when Edward paid the taxi driver in front of the motel. He was so tired that he almost staggered. The man offered to help him to his room, but Edward waved him away.

Jon and Nancy were just putting their last suitcase in their station wagon. Eddie was already asleep in the back.

"Hi, Dad. We didn't expect you back yet. We left a note for you," Nancy said.

"We were too excited to settle down, so we thought we would drive while Eddie is asleep," Jon added. "We will get a motel by Disneyland. Maybe we can sleep then."

"Good idea. I'm bushed. I'll sleep a few hours and then head straight home."

"Where is Grace?"

"Still at the reception with Gary. They will drive north together, by way of Reno, I would imagine," he said grinning.

"Great!" Jon helped Nancy into the car and shut the door. "That's good, Dad."

"Why didn't you tell me the reason she wouldn't marry him, son?"

"It was her business, Dad. I agree that you need someone to take care of you."

"No, Jon. Not any more. I'll make it on my own, with God's help. Grace deserves her own happiness. She has given herself to us all her life. Dear Grace!"

"How about Mom now, after all of this?"

"She will never come back, son."

"I'm not so sure. Her obsession is with Aurora. What happens when Aurora doesn't want her anymore?"

"She seems to have plenty of men around to take care of her."

"Yeah, I guess she does. We'd better get going. Get some rest, Dad. We'll see you at home in a few days. I still have some vacation days coming. After we see Disneyland, we plan to take our time driving up the coast. By the way, any chance of just you and me getting to Grand Canyon this summer?"

"Could be, son," he said smiling and remembering their earlier trip.

Nancy threw him a kiss as they drove off.

Edward locked the door of the motel behind him. Grace had her key. He took off his rented tuxedo and hung it on the special hangers by Jon's.

He stretched out on the opened couch and covered himself. In his mind a kaleidoscope of color, picture, and light danced. His body ached, but his soul was amazingly free. Whatever the future brought, he could face it.

When Grace tiptoed in several hours later, he was

sleeping peacefully. She waited to wake him until Gary carried out her suitcases. then she went to him and kissed him.

"Daddy?"

"Yes, love."

"Is it okay if Gary and I go home by way of Reno? You see, we have had enough of weddings to last a lifetime. Would you mind, Daddy, if you didn't marry us?"

Gary came and put his arm around her. "You know I will always take care of her, sir."

Edward stood up and hugged them both. "You know I want nothing more than happiness for you both. Gary, this has been my hope for a long time. God bless you both."

"One thing, Dad. Could you go by the church and get my red dressing case and my clothes? It is so early; I'm sure the place wouldn't be open yet."

"Won't you need those things?"

"Gary says I can buy anything I need. 'Bye, Daddy. Thank you. I love you." She kissed him again, and they left in a flurry of excitement.

Edward sank back onto the couch, trying to get comfortable. The outdoor sounds were muted, and the semi-darkness and strangeness of the place closed in around him.

I am finally alone, he told himself. He wondered if he would ever get used to it.

There was one more item of business he must face— Julia. Some day soon he had to settle everything between them. He couldn't sleep. Bits and pieces of their lives surfaced in fast succession. Bittersweet memories.

A compelling urge overwhelmed him. He wanted to be home. He wanted to be surrounded by familiar things.

He got up and dressed. Grace had packed most of his things for him. He finished and went to check out. The sleepy manager grumbled at him, but Edward induced him with an extra big tip to return the tuxedos.

It was still too early to pick up Grace's things. A brightly lit cafe drew his attention. He parked the car and ate a leisurely breakfast, amazed at how hungry he was.

He began to think of the business of his church. This was Sunday morning, and his people would soon be gathering. He loved each of them, and now he would be free to serve them in a new way. It was exciting to think of the possibilities. Maybe he would stay there after all.

The waitress filled his coffee cup again.

His thoughts were warm and pleasant. His stomach felt better than it had for ages.

Grace and Gary. This was their wedding day. He would like to be with them, but it was much better this way.

He let Julia intrude into his thoughts. He must learn to put her in a special place and pray for her in love whenever he thought of her. He knew it would take time, and he knew he would never go through with a divorce. If that was to be, she would have to do it.

It was still early when he arrived at the church. There was activity at the side door. A cleaning crew was working frantically to remove the last signs of the wedding before the Sunday crowd would arrive.

Edward went past them and down the steps to the lower auditorium. On a table by the door were the things left from the wedding: clothing, cosmetics, a hair dryer. He found Grace's red leather case and her clothes.

When he reached the top of the steps he felt compelled to look once more into the sanctuary. God had met him there, and the memory was sweet.

He stepped through the heavy doors. The early morning sun streamed through the great stained glass window in a myriad of brilliant colors. The Christ, hands outstretched, was illuminated with glorious light.

Edward dropped Grace's things in a back pew and went slowly down the aisle. He couldn't take his eyes from that light. It penetrated his deepest being with joy and glory.

The silence was broken by sobbing. He turned, his eyes adjusting to the dimness. It was Julia! She was sitting where she had been during the ceremony. She had her face covered with her hands and was crying in deep, painful sobs. Her hair was disheveled, her orchid corsage crushed, her wine velvet dress stained and torn.

"Julia."

"Go away! Why did you come here?"

"What are you doing here?" He sat beside her.

"I have no place to go."

"What? Look at me."

She glanced up. Her face was red and swollen, her eyes bloodshot, her make-up smeared. "I have no place to go."

"But . . . your apartment . . ."

"I gave it up. I thought Aurora . . ." She was sobbing again.

"Julia?"

"I thought Aurora would have a place for me with her. She . . . she . . . told me . . . to . . . to go away . . . to get lost . . ."

"Now stop, Julia. You will be sick."

"I am sick. I want to die. I came here to pray for God to let me die . . ."

He pulled her to him and wiped her face with his handkerchief. She didn't pull away. "It is not the end for you, Julia. You have the rest of us."

"I went to help her dress to leave on her honeymoon. She was horrible. She told me she didn't need me a minute longer. She has a personal maid, a hair dresser, a wardrobe mistress . . . and on and on. She told me to leave her alone. She told me I had always tried to run her life . . ."

There was much more, and Edward let her say it all. It was painful and horrible, bitter and hateful. He only half-listened, praying that he would have the words to ease the pain in her mind and heart.

Finally she stopped, exhausted. He knew she had been up all night and here in the church for hours. She was shivering and weak.

"Come, Julia. Let me take you and get you something hot to drink. Where is your coat?"

"Come? Come?" She stood and looked at him, her eyes staring. "I can't. Never!"

"Of course you can. I am your husband."

"That's just it. I've . . . I . . . you . . . you couldn't want me . . ."

"Julia, listen to me." He put his hands on her shoulders and shook her gently. "I do not care what you have done or how you have lived. I love you. I forgive you. I don't want to hear about any of it, ever. I want you. Do you hear me?"

"You. . .love. . .me?"

He touched the pearls at her throat. "Yes, Julia, I love you." He realized that he could not have said those words sincerely a few hours earlier.

She shook her head in disbelief, rubbing her hands on her hips against her skirt. She backed away from him.

He followed, hands outstretched.

They stood. Then she reached a trembling hand toward him. He took it between both of his.

"Come." He led her by the hand up the aisle. They knelt and prayed together, asking God to restore their trust. He knew it would be a long time before she was well again; but God had given her back to him to love and cherish, and he was filled with thanksgiving.

Someday, in God's time, his prayers for Aurora would also be answered.

He believed in his heart that it wasn't too late—not for him, not for Julia . . . and not for Aurora.